THE PALE COLD LIGHT

/ / / /

J.R. RAIN

STANDALONE NOVELS

All the Way Back Home
Winter Wind
Silent Echo
The Body Departed
The Grail Quest
Elvis Has *Not* Left the Building
The Lost Ark

Published by
Crop Circle Books
212 Third Crater, Moon

Printed in the United States of America.

ISBN- 9781678318734

Chapter One

It is windy and cold and there is rain, too.

Not a lot of rain, but enough. Enough to make him think he may never be warm again. Warmth is a luxury. He knows that now. He didn't know that before. He knows a lot of things now. A lot of terrible and wonderful things.

He pushes through the dusting of rain and keeps his head down and the weight off his disfigured ankle. He keeps the weight off by pushing a shopping cart that, even to this day, works surprisingly well. A gift to him, surely. A gift from God.

He loves God and will never stop loving God, not now nor ever, no matter what happens.

And a lot has happened.

Thank you, God, for my life, my clothing, my cart with its oiled wheels. Thank you, God, for the breath in my chest.

He ducks his head against the wind and maneuvers around the broken sidewalk, and breathes through the scarf that covers his lips and nose—especially his nose—a scarf given to him by an elderly woman a day or so ago. Maybe a week ago. She'd gotten out of her car and wrapped the scarf around him as he crossed the street in the crosswalk. He heard her words again, and had started repeating them often, as he did now:

"You are loved. Never forget that. You are loved."

He looks back often for his dog and calls to her until he remembers that she died in his arms not too long ago. He reminds himself now, again, but he looks anyway, just in case. Maybe she didn't die. Maybe she had died and come back. Maybe she had gotten better. Maybe he had forgotten what happened. Maybe he was thinking of another dog. Maybe he made it all up.

Maybe, maybe, maybe.

Maybe another dog would come, as she had, years ago, to comfort him. He looks back again, but no. He looks again, this time faster, and almost trips, but she is still not there. He looks again and again, and thinks he sees her, but it is a shadow. Maybe. He will check later. Yes, maybe she would come back from wherever she had gone off to. She would come back to him where she belongs. Her name is Blessed, and he misses her all over again, and cries for her all over again, the tears lost on his cheeks in the rain.

Maybe he would see her again in his dreams. Boy, he sure does love Blessed. Never knew a dog like her. Always by his side, a friend to the end. He likes friends. He likes people who are nice to him too. He likes people who smile and nod and think of him as a person. He likes to be thought of as a person. He knows he is dirty and talks to himself too much. He thinks everyone talks to themselves, but most people do it alone at home, or in the shower, or in the car. Except he doesn't have a shower or a home or a car, and so he talks to himself on the street, his home for now. Or in the park, his home for now. Or under the bridge, his home for now. Or in the shelter, which is his favorite home of all.

He knows his mind is lost. He knows he can't think one thought for very long at all. He knows this and he does not care because this is the way God made him and he loves God more than himself. God has been so good to him. God has blessed him with life and he loves life and so he loves God.

He loves the cold because he loves to be warm too.

He loves smiles because they remind him of God.

He loves angry people because he knows life is hard. He tells them that God loves them, and sometimes the words come out right and sometimes they don't. Sometimes the words sound wrong to his ears, too, and he wonders when he last spoke. Days, sometimes weeks.

But sometimes he will go whole days where he does nothing but speak to himself. He likes his voice, even if he can't understand what he is saying. He knows what he means to say and that's all that matters. His mind isn't right and he knows that but some minds don't have to be right, right? Some can be wrong. And all are from God and he loves God more than he loves himself.

He wonders what he says, but then he forgets what he is wondering, and people look at him more and he smiles at their frowns and tells them God loves them. He hopes people can see God in him. Some days he knows that God is with him, walking next to him, holding his hand. He can feel God there. He feels it and knows it.

Where is Blessed?

His cart squeaks but he is so very thankful for the cart. Whoever made it has to be a genius. The metal. The curved bars. The hundreds and hundreds of tiny welds. The perfect symmetry of the whole beautiful thing. It wasn't off balance. It was made to help people carry their groceries. It wasn't made for him, he knows. It was made for a grocery store and he worries that he has sinned, but didn't he find it behind a dumpster with a half filled can of Coke that was more delicious than anything he had ever drank in all his life? He had, and he doesn't think it is a sin to find things. He wishes he could ask his mother if it is a sin, but she is gone to heaven, too, with Blessed.

And someone else, someone else, someone else. A young one. A sweetheart. A precious angel.

No. No. No.

Stop. Stop.

Good. Good.

Better.

He pauses, breathes, braces himself.

It is coming on evening and he knows he needs to find a place to sleep, but he would like to eat, too, although he is less hopeful about eating. He can't remember when he last ate.

He pauses, thinks, but nope, he can't remember.

He continues on, shuffling, pushing the cart, putting weight on the side of his foot where no weight belongs. His foot hurts. So does his ankle. So does his stomach. His stomach hurts most of all.

He pauses now and bows his head and feels the wave of panic grip him because he thinks there is a very real chance that he may never eat again, and with his head bowed he thanks the Lord for the food he has provided in the past, and if he is to never to eat again, he understands. More food for others. He likes the idea of others eating, if it's not him. His stomach hurts. The pain, the pain...

He continues on and finds tears on his cheeks.

A woman watches him and shakes her head, and he hears her say something about being pathetic. And he smiles and thanks God that she is healthy and alive and dressed warm and smells good.

The pain grips him again, a long, slow, sad, throbbing pain.

His stomach is like a child alone in the forest, alone and afraid and forgotten. He puts his hand on his stomach and tells it everything will be okay because God is good.

Sometimes he eats well, sometimes he will find a whole meal thrown aside, a half a chicken in a dumpster. Sometimes an angel will buy him a meal while he sits with his dog and looks toward the sun. Sometimes the shelter will give him a hot meal. But the pain always returns, often within hours or days. Sometimes the pain in his stomach is so great that he finds himself weeping in agony, because the child is lost and hungry and he doesn't know what to do for it.

But then he prays and asks for forgiveness because he was weak and doubtful and God is great.

Sometimes angels stop and ask if they can help and he always points to his dog first and says he is hungry. Sometimes the angels feed his dog, and sometimes they feed him, too. Angels, he knows, are real.

Blessed.

He looks back, but she is not there and his heart breaks all over again and he wonders if Blessed is in Heaven with God, and if she has enough to eat, and if someone is taking good care of her, and if her tail is wagging, and if she is happier without him.

He pauses because his mind is spinning again. It always spins when he thinks of Blessed, it spins and spins, and he can't see or think and all he feels is loss and fear and worry and hunger. He holds onto his shopping cart with dirty hands and feels the tears and knows his mind might never come back, ever, and he wills it to come back, it has to come back, if his minds goes, then there will be nothing left of him, and he will be gone, gone, gone.

He breathes and grips the cart and feels a hand on his back and hears an angel's voice talking to him, now holding his arm. And now the angel is patting his hands, and he thinks this is the first time anyone has touched him in days, weeks, maybe years.

When he opens his eyes again, he feels the tears on his face and the drool in his beard, and the angel is gone and he is alone again on the broken sidewalk with cars passing and people looking at him and shaking their heads. He grips his shopping cart. He doesn't remember what just happened or where the daylight went, but he remembers his dog in heaven, and fights another wave of dizziness that threatens to tear his mind away, but he holds on, holds on, holds on.

And continues forward.

Evening is coming, and so is the cold wind. He huddles within the many layers of clothing he's been blessed with. He wonders where he will sleep and if he will eat tonight. If he doesn't sleep or eat, he is okay with that too.

He wonders if the angry man will be at the park again, the angry man who had yelled at the crying woman. The angry man in the long black jacket who had taken the woman away, by the hand, deeper into the woods behind the park. He hopes the angry man isn't so angry anymore, and he hopes the girl is done crying and is happy again. He hopes they ate good today and sat together and held hands and remembered that God loves them. He loves them, too, wherever they are.

He turns into the park and heads down a slight incline, pushing the cart, and dragging his damaged foot.

Chapter Two

Blessed.

He'd buried her in the park a few nights ago. He'd dug through the mulch and grass and roots and blackberry vines and little worms. He'd used the edge of his hands and scraped up huge chunks of soil. His hands bled. He had spent the past few days picking the dirt and splinters out from under his nails, all while he looked for his doggie, all while wondering where the dirt and splinters had come from.

He wants nothing more than to sit by the grave of his Blessed, if he can find it. Yes, he remembers where he buried her, behind the trash can and twisted tree. He had placed a marker there. Or so he thinks he did. He is pretty sure he is to look for a branch in the ground. A branch with lots of leaves.

Once down in the park, he eases the shopping cart into a cozy nook between handicapped parking and the curb. He thinks the carts fit there perfectly, as if the space had been made just for his cart. He looks back once at the cart and smiles. He looks back again for his doggie, too, but remembers she is dead, and he does not think he will ever look back for her again.

He walks across the grass and misses the steadiness of his cart. He lost his cane a few months ago, although he suspects it was stolen. It had been a fine cane he himself had found leaning against a trash can. The person who stole his cane was surely in worse shape than he is. He is glad they stole it and he hopes they have made good use of it. Maybe someday he will find another cane. Until then, he has his cart.

Except here on the grass where the cart didn't roll so good.

As that thought passes through his mind, he begins looking around for a tree branch and sees one almost instantly. It is all he can do to lean down and pick it up without falling, balancing most of his weight on his one good foot. The ground is uneven and he wobbles and sways and he thinks he might fall but something invisible—surely God—keeps him on his one good leg and now his reaching fingers grab hold of the thick branch. It is a fine branch, still covered in green needles and twigs and off-shoots.

It is also about the right height, too, and he tests it, putting in a little weight on it. It bends but does not break and this is enough for him to smile for the first time all day.

He moves through the park with his new cane, proud and alive and happy for the first time in a week or so, ever since Blessed died in his arms after panting and not drinking all day. The sun is setting, and he needs to make sure he can see the ground because the woods behind the park are dark and not seeing the ground is what caused him to break his ankle in the first place, years ago.

Yes, definitely years ago. Maybe just two years ago. Last year, at least.

He hobbles over the sloping grass and down toward a dark path that leads to where he buried Blessed. More interestingly, he knows this is where the angry man had taken the crying woman last night. This is where he heard them make naked, as he thinks of it, because he cannot get himself to say make love or sex. And he most certainly can't get himself to say any swear words. Swear words are offensive to his ears, and offensive to God's ears most of all, and he cringes when he hears them and replaces them in his mind with words that are nicer.

As the angry man pulled the woman by the hand down into the woods behind the park, the woman had stumbled and falled. Felled? Fellen?

He feels the panic rise in him until the word 'fallen' appears in his thoughts and this settles him down again. He doesn't like to lose words. He's lost so many words. He doesn't want to lose fallen, too.

From his bench, he watched the angry man yank the woman to her feet and disappear into the trees, where they made naked noises. The naked noises turned into screams, then choking noises. Then gurgling noises. Then nothing. Then, later, the sound of scraping or digging, some grunting. This went on for some time. He thinks it is similar to the sounds he made when he dug a grave for Blessed with his bare hands.

A little while later the man had emerged alone from the woods. The man wiped his hands on his jeans. His hands were covered in dirt. The man had looked around briefly, wildly, but had mostly kept his head down. The man continued up the path and out of the park, and never once did the man think to look back at the bench.

That had been last night. He had awakened in the freezing cold, the drool on his face nearly frozen. There had been people already walking in the park but most avoided him and all looked away. He smiled at them anyway.

He was pretty sure he had dreamed of the angry man and crying woman.

Now, the grassy slope gave way to low ferns and narrow trails and thick trees that rose higher than skyscrapers. He moved off the trail and did his best to move over rocks and roots and twists and turns. The naked sounds, the whimpering, the choking, the digging, came from around here. He's sure of it. Okay, maybe not sure of it. He hasn't really been sure of anything in a long time, except for his love for God and Blessed.

This is also where he buried Blessed.

He had carried her here and buried her with his own hands, dragging great heaps of dirt and leaves and branches and rocks, using his hands as a sort of drudge. He doesn't know where he knows the word drudge but it feels right to him.

He hadn't dug very deep. The forest floor had been veritably covered with debris, so many leaves and branches and moss and dead ferns and rotted tree trunks. It had been so easy to use the debris to cover his dog, along with the loose dirt, and he had done a good job building a mound for her, and packing the dirt and debris around the mound, so that she was safe and happy and comfortable. And he had sat next to that mound for the rest of that night, and into the next day, and when he finally stood because he was hungry, he had forgotten why he was sitting next to the mound. And later that day, as he looked for Blessed and didn't see her, the panic had begun, and then he had lost his mind, he knew, for many days thereafter. He had lost a week or more. He was sure of it.

He is on the right path now, he is sure of it. Yes, this is where he had buried Blessed. He thinks.

No, he knows.

There is the trash can, yes, and there is the twisted tree, yes, and there is the small mound with the tree branch marker. He is sad and he is happy. But mostly he is sad.

He wants nothing more than to sit with Blessed and to sleep next to her grave.

He hobbles closer and closer, faster and faster... and sees something else.

Another mound, maybe ten feet away. It's bigger and not nearly as neat.

Something is reaching out from it. Something pale and small and twisted.

It is, he is certain, a human hand.

***

He had long since dug her out.

She was, he knows, the girl who had been crying last night, the girl who had been making noises, then made choking noises. He can see the bruising around her throat. Her eyes were open, but he closed them because she looked scared and in pain and he felt sorry for her. Her mouth was open too, probably trying to breathe or scream for help.

But it was when he looked into her mouth —a mouth partially filled with dirt and debris— that something happened to him. More than the shock of seeing a dead woman (he had seen many dead people on the streets, dead from natural causes and even murder), it was the bloodied gap in her upper front row of teeth that rocked his world.

She was missing a tooth.

That had been hours ago. Now, as the sky lightened and the first joggers appeared, his broken mind clicked on again, and with it came the certainty he had seen something like this before. Not something... someone. Someone close to him.

With that certainty, his mind spins off again.

Spins and spins and spins.

Chapter Three

There are some things he knows for sure:

His love for God and his love for Blessed. His empty stomach. Hard to ignore that. And the pain in his broken ankle. Hard to ignore that too. There are some things he is only vaguely sure of: the month or year, and when he ate last. And then there are some things he's not so sure about: his memory, primarily, but also if he was speaking or thinking.

That was a tough one. Often when he thought he was thinking, he was speaking. And sometimes when he thought he speaking, he was thinking. Both of which caused confusion and alarm in others.

It caused confusion and alarm in him, too.

Now, he needed to be sure of that which he was least sure about: speaking and his memory. After all, the police were questioning him, asking him over and over about what he saw, who he saw, what he heard, what he found, how he found it.

First, they marched him, stumbling and tripping, over to the flashing police cruisers which had driven right up to the wooded area. Then they threw him against the first squad car, and demanded to know why he'd killed the woman. He tried to answer but couldn't get his mouth to work. As he searched for words, one kicked his ankle. He cried out and fell over as another pulled him back up and threw him over the hood.

As they pat him down, he thanks them for reasons he cannot remember, and weeps because the woman is dead and so is Blessed. He is calling out to his dog as they yell at him more. He cries harder because he has never felt so sad in all his life.

No, he thinks as the police finally back off. I have been sadder.

Except he doesn't know when or why he'd been so sad, but a hint of the memory is there in his damaged mind. It wants to come to the surface, but it's been buried deep. He gives up trying to find it.

One of the officers is in his face again and talking really loud and his breath smells bad and he doesn't know what the officer wants from him. The man's words and spittle and breath make him nervous and he loses control of his bladder and stands there and knows he wet himself and is ashamed and scared and now the officer is disgusted and yelling some more. A woman appears, pushing the men away. She has kind eyes.

The woman takes his hand and leads him around the squad car. He feels the urine in his shoe. She walks slowly, and he sees her looking at his twisted ankle. She makes small, sympathetic sounds as he limps around the car with her.

She opens the door to the back seat, and he feels an old fear come over him and he shakes his head. He doesn't want to go into a police car again. He doesn't want to be arrested again. He doesn't know what to say or how to defend himself, but he doesn't want to go to jail again, even for a night. No, not at all. Not for a night. No, no, no. He shakes his head and doesn't know if he is speaking or not, but then remembers the woman in the ground and her cold hand and feels sadness for her and soon he stops shaking his head.

"It's alright. I just want you to take some

weight off that ankle. Have a seat. I promise, we're just going to talk."

The woman speaks these words while looking him directly in his eyes, that's how it feels, too. He hears them but he sees her eyes and she seems kind and patient, and he feels safe with her, and so he sinks down into the backseat. She smiles and nods and moves around the cruiser and soon she is opening the door on the other side and sliding onto the seat next to him. She has a shiny badge on her hip and she is dressed nice and smells of coffee and shampoo. He knows he smells of piss and dirt and terrible body odor, but she does not comment on it. He imagines her scent nullifying his scent. Maybe, just maybe there is no smell at all, he thinks. Her hair is pulled back so tight it looks like it hurts.

"It doesn't hurt," she says, smiling.

Now he realizes he spoke those last words, maybe a lot of words. Maybe all of the words.

"What is your name?" she asks.

And some things he can never remember. Like his name. Or where he came from. His parents. His age. His middle name. His last name. His parents or brothers and sisters, if he had any. Where he was born. If he had kids or if he was ever married.

But the "not remembering his name" part is

hardest. He feels ashamed and saddened and scared.

"It's okay," she says, and reaches out and touches the back of his hand, and he is certain that it is the first time anyone has touched him on purpose, without hurting him or stealing from him or arresting him or recoiling and wiping their hands either. She touched him and left her fingers there on the back of his brownish hand. He can't remember if his skin has always been this brown or if he's just dirty. "You should hear me trying to remember my children's name. I go through all of them forward and backward before I find the right one. Don't worry about it."

He doesn't know what she's talking about but he is happy she has children who delight her. He is pretty sure he never had children, but he thinks maybe he did. Maybe one. Or two. Or none. Lots of dogs, though. Lots and lots of dogs.

The words "one daughter" appears in his thoughts. The thought feels right, but he doesn't know why it feels right.

Meanwhile, the nice lady steps away and tells the others to leave him alone. One of them wants to "bring him in" for questioning but the nice lady who touched his hand said she got all the answers she could from him, and she had

looked back at him and almost smiled. Almost.
It was a nice almost-smile.

The dead woman... he'd held her hand all
night. He had sat with her and cried for her, and
looked at her damaged face and broken body
and... felt a need to do something. He didn't
know what. That something had bothered him
all night until now, until now, until now.

Now, he wanted answers. Now, he wanted
whoever did this to her. He knew how to find
killers, didn't he? Didn't he? Yes, he did. The
memory comes back to him with shocking
clarity. He gasps, shakes his head, clutching the
seat cushions next to him. The police, the
police, the police...

He was one of them. Or had been. Or was
he now still? No, a long time ago. One of them.
No, not quite. Something else, something else.
The word "detective" appears in his thoughts.

Detective first grade.

The memories.

The memories.

Oh, yes. Detective first grade. Seattle. A
detective, and a damn good one.

No, not him.

Yes, him. No, no. no... someone else.

The memories. So many... more than he can
believe. Flooding back now.

A long time ago. Another life ago. Was it

him? Or was it his old man? The tall man with the dark mustache who wore the slacks and white dress shirt and polished shoes, and who wore the badge and the shoulder holster with the department-issued gun. He had a partner, many partners, and solved crimes, many crimes, so good at it. No, great at it. But his case... his daughter's case.

Too much, too much, too much.

He can't think about that now. No one should see what he saw. No one. Ever. Never. No. No. No. His daughter, dead, in his arms, the blood, the blood... so much blood.

He remembers the sobbing—his sobbing. Never could he stop. Night and day, awake and asleep. He'd felt himself losing his mind, felt it all slipping away, was so thankful to lose it, so thankful to forget. How long, he doesn't know. A long, long, long time ago. Never did he want to remember.

But he remembers now.

The dead woman in the park, her missing tooth, her broken body, the shallow grave. All the same, he was sure of it.

His daughter? He had a daughter? He did, he was sure of it. He'd found her. So broken and ruined and discarded, worse than any case he'd ever seen.

Something had broken in him. Something

had snapped in his mind. He'd felt it instantly, highly aware of it, and he'd known he was done, and that's when the hallucinations started. He remembers the first ones. He remembers seeing his daughter alive and happy and talking to him, and he smiled and talked back to her and people looked at him oddly, especially his partner, and many people spoke to him and talked to him and he'd found himself in a hospital where he'd been given drugs... but with the drugs, the memories returned and he knew he had to stop the drugs and knew he had to escape, and so he did.

He'd waited for the nurse to leave. He'd caught the door before it fully shut. He had listened at the door. He slipped through when all was quiet. He kept slipping through, door after door, until he was outside and running and running. As he ran, he forgot more and more, and found peace even as he lost his mind. Bye mind, bye memories, he didn't need them or want them.

So long ago. Another life ago. It was not him, no, no, no.

But it was. He is sure of it.

His eyes snap open. Finds himself alone on a park bench. The police are gone. It is coming on evening.

"Yes," he says to no one, sitting up. "It was

me."
It was me.
I am he.
"Me."

Chapter Four

Days later, I think.

It is morning, and the breeze is cool on my face and I notice for the first time the length of my beard. How did it get so long? I run my finger through it and pull at it and wonder if it's really there or if I am imagining it.

The painful tangles remind me it is real. I brush them out as I sit straighter. The breeze, the morning sun, the pain in my foot, the birds overhead, the cold in my bones and the hunger in my belly... all real.

So real...

So real, real, real, real, real.

So... fucking... real.

Goddamn motherfucking real.

I'm here. I'm really here. This is me. Here in this place, in this now, in this body, in this mind, in these clothes, in this skin.

My dog... my dog... God, no. Please. Where is she? Where is she? No, God no. My sweet dog. Please, no...

Gone. Buried. With my own hands.

My breath catches, lungs burn. I cough, breathe, cough.

The sun, so bright...

I roll over and fall to a knee. I'd been curled up on a crate in an... alley? Yes, an alley. That's what they call these dark, smelly, safe, dangerous, quiet, painful, deadly places between the places that we lurk and live and dance and sleep and feed and fuck and die...

Father... my Father... my heavenly Father.

You heard me. You heard me. Thank you, Father, for hearing me.

I breathe and cough, and up comes a vile liquid from down deep.

Now, a deep, glorious breath.

My dog... where is she... dead. She's dead.

No, please, no.

Yes, many days now.

No. Many weeks.

I remember. Lying at my feet all night, panting, licking my hand, panting and struggling for breath, and I struggled for breath, too, and I held her as she licked my hand, and then the licking stopped, and so did her breathing. My sweet girl.

Gone. I know this. I know this.

She is not next to me, not down the alley, not foraging for food, not growling at those who would hurt me, not sleeping by my feet.

Gone. Deaded. *Dead.*

I miss her, miss her, miss. God bless her. Blessed.

Thank you, Father. Thank you for giving her to me for a few years.

I miss her and I love her. And I hope she is happy with you now. Please let her be happy and safe.

Buried... with my own hands. In the forest. Where I found the girl.

The girl...

I sit back, head spinning, thoughts spinning, world spinning.

Breathe, relax. Who am I? I don't know, yes you do. Relax, relax, good.

She was kilt—killed—last night. No, a few nights ago. Killed. Murdered. Strangled. I'd heard it. Heard it. Did I see it? No. I saw the man. The fucking man. The piece of shit who hurt her so bad.

I hold my head in both hands and breathe and think and see and smile and laugh and cry a little, no, a lot. Something is happening, something, something.

I lay my head back down and sleep and the world passes me by. I hear voices and cars and laughter and barking and bad brakes and feel the wind and sun and rain, and many more days have passed me by.

Many days.

Many, many days.

And each time I awaken, I sit up and stumble to the nearby drinking fountain and stumble to the nearby bathroom. People watch and ignore me all at once. I expect this. I expect to be watched and ignored and pitied and feared and loathed and ridiculed. Truth is, it ain't so bad. I got used to it. I even got used to the random beatings and attacks, from other homeless, from rowdy teens, from drunks, from ice cold killers, from cops, from roaming groups, from a woman with a bat, from dogs, from raccoons, from rats, from friends, from enemies, from the rich and the poor. The beatings came often. The beatings hurt, yes. The beatings scarred me physically. I am certain they scarred me emotionally, but I didn't use such words then. I simply understood the beatings broke me open, inside and out, within and without.

The words "no brainer" appear in my thoughts.

"No brainer," I whisper to myself. It is a word or words, a concept, I haven't used in a long time. I say the words, again and again, my voice is ragged and raw, empty and alive.

I find myself standing at the little water fountain in front of the Catholic church. I close my eyes and listen to the splashing and the gurgling, and smile. My thoughts... flowing, with ease, like the water, like this fountain. Like water over the land, and down hills into ponds and lakes and oceans.

I sit and think and the sun slips behind the nearby buildings. I open and close my hand, look down at my broken ankle, look up at the fading skies, and back behind me, but she is gone. My sweet girl is gone.

But she is not the only one gone, right?

I had another sweet girl.

A daughter.

Murdered.

Chapter Five

It is the next day, and I am in bed.

Or, rather, in the cot I'm provided with. The cot is stiff and narrow, but it is softer than a bench or the concrete, but not as soft as a pile of boxes or a pile of clothing. Now, a pile of clothing on boxes... heaven.

This is neither, but it is off the ground and is clean and is in a clean place, even if the place is loud and disturbing and even a little frightening.

Despite a night filled with howling, sobbing, screaming, two fistfights, and an unusually high amount of mumbling, I awake feeling good, if not tired. With that thought in mind, I decide to make earplugs. I couldn't remember the word for them last night, as I lay listening to a woman singing "Purple Rain" over and over. The thing was... she could really sing, so I didn't mind it so much.

Still... earplugs. Yes. Chewing gum works, as I've learned.

Now, I roll out of the cot, and nearly fall when my left ankle slides out from under me. My broken and twisted left ankle. I catch myself on the corner of the cot, gasp at the shooting pain.

I stare down at the twisted abomination. I have only a vague memory of breaking it...

A car had hit me. I'd been panhandling... somewhere. Sitting on a curb, next to a flower bed. A car veered toward me, continued coming at me. I saw a brief flash of the man grinning behind the wheel. No, he was laughing. He was also alone. I scrambled. Not in time. His tire caught my left foot, rolled over it, breaking it. I'd screamed as the car continued on. No one stopped to help. I'd crawled back into the flower bed until the police came and told me to leave, and so I had, pushing my cart, holding my broken ankle up, hopping along, until I passed out again from the pain.

The sock is filthy beyond description. I have discarded hundreds of ruined socks. Time to throw this one away too. I'll find another.

Funny how socks always pop up. Maybe they escape from dryers. Shoes do not fit over my disfigured foot. Socks only. The thicker the better.

I ease back down on the cot and pull this one off and study my foot for the first time in years. There is scar tissue where the break occurred. It had been a compound fracture, with some of my bone sticking out for months until the skin finally healed over. Although the break had mended, it had done so at a stomach turning angle. More of a u-shape than anything. Which is why I walk on the side of my foot. At present, my foot is swollen and red and damaged, the outside covered in callouses. It looks more like a twisted root than a foot.

I sigh, wad up the ruined sock up, and hop to my good foot. I stuff the sock in my jacket pocket. I would throw it out later. For now, I am hungry, and I can smell food in the shelter's kitchen. Mercy, but I was hungry.

I hobble forward, wishing I had a cane, or my shopping cart, but I'm making do.

Thank you, God, for the people who run this shelter and opening their doors to the likes of me. Thank you, God, for the air I breathe and the life you have given me.

Amen.

Chapter Six

Depth and breadth. Beauty and sunshine. An awakening. Light and ocean. Lifts his face —my face—to the sun. The sky, beauty, smiles. Lift off. Soaring. Lightness. Epic. Beauty. Determination.

The moment is fleeting. A short window of clarity. Yes, this I know. Must act now. Now, now, now.

Already feeling the insanity returning. Too soon. Need more time.

Please.

A race against his mind—*my* mind.

Slipping. Slipping.

Need to move. Need to act. A race. A chase. He can do this. I can do this. I. Me. I have to do this. For her. For her. For her. For all of them. Please, Father, give me one more week. One more day. One more hour. I will find him. I will find him.

I will find him...

Chapter Seven

I shake my head.

Wow. Okay. Breathe. I'm back, I'm back, I'm back.

Where did I go? I don't know. My mind. Yes, my mind.

I find myself standing at a railing, looking out over the Sound. The sun is high above, and hot, and I am sweating in my layered clothing. Too much clothing. Need it, don't need it. Leave some, find some. I fidget, feeling a familiar anxiousness. But what if I never find another coat? This coat... I love this coat. It's been good to me. Almost a friend. I don't need it. Now now. Maybe later. I turn, don't see my shopping cart. Where did I leave it? Where,

where? I panic, nearly weep, but don't.

The alley. I left it in the alley. Which alley? I don't remember. I will find it. No, leave it behind. How will I walk? I look down and see a tree branch. Gnarled and twisted. Ah, that's how I got here. I remember. The cart is easier, yes. The cart is my home, my room, a traveling bedroom. But they do not allow carts at the shelter. That's right, that's right. I knew this and left mine behind in an alley.

Which alley, which alley, think, think, think...

Not far from here. Where is here?

I grip the tree branch, turn, nearly fall.

Pikes Place Market. I am outdoors, near a railing, the view of the Sound and the Ferris Wheel and the cruise ships and the cranes and Alki Beach and condos and water and the islands and sky, so much sky.

I feel the sweat, smell the stink.

My jacket. My amazing perfect blessed jacket. A gift from God. Everything is a gift from God.

I step away from the railing, balancing on my good foot, my bad one lifted up off the ground, touching the cement but with no weight. I pull the zipper tab of my jacket. It glides smoothly, making a zippery sound. I wonder if the sound it makes is why they named it a zipper. It sure makes a *zzzzip* type of sound.

I pull the tab all the way down and fresh air, cool air, blessed air fills me up, moving inside my jacket like a living thing. Now I shrug out of my jacket. First time in days, maybe weeks, maybe months.

Ah, my sweet jacket. My friend in the cold.

But it is too hot now. The jacket is too thick. It is also very dirty. Maybe the dirtiest thing to ever exist in the city ever. Maybe the whole world. I shrug it off, or try to but it doesn't go willingly, no, it is a part of me. It is me. My second skin. My life. My whole world sometimes. I am safe in that jacket, even though it is also caked with my own dried blood.

It falls free from my shoulders and I catch it in a loop in my arm. Wow, so heavy. So perfect, so dirty, so smelly, but I love it. Love it. Love it.

I can't do it. But I know I must.

A shift, pulling, releasing, knowing.

It's time for a change. I need to be a different person to do what I have to do. I need to look different, too. I need to sound different. I need to smell different. I need to think differently. The jacket.

"My yesterday," I whisper to myself. Or do I think it?

Too warm. It's okay. I don't need it. The

sun. Yes, the perfect sun.

My skin soaks in the sun, the wind, the cool air on my sweaty, reddish, dirty skin.

I turn, look for a trash can. There, there.

I grab my branch. I picked a good one. A sturdy one. Surely another gift from God. I smile as I approach the trash can. There is a woman approaching it too, and I smile at her and she does not smile and turns away. That's okay. God is love. She is love. I am love. I continue smiling as she hurries away, looking once over her shoulder. I smile at her with love. She is a good person. I am a good person. We are good people.

I lift the domed trash can lid off. I do it like an expert, and I laugh at this. I am an expert. The trash is a beautiful thing. So much food, clothing, and life in trash cans. God bless these cans.

But I do not search. My belly is full. My skin is cool. My heart is heavy and light. Sadness and death and eagerness and revenge. It is all in there, but for now, I do not think about what's inside the trash can. For now. I think of my new self. The new me to help the old me.

I stand at the trash can and forget why I am there. The sun, yes. The wind, yes. The heat, yes. My coat, my coat. My blessed coat.

Goodbye old friend.

I love you and the hugs you have given me and the softness you have provided and the warmth you have given. You gave and gave and gave.

Goodbye. Goodbye.

Goodbye.

I shove the coat down into the trash can and look away, tears in my eyes, my jaw shaking, knowing I am crying, knowing people are looking at me. I hang onto my branch and place the dome carefully over the trash can and wipe my tears and hold on to my branch with both hands.

I stare down at the trash as a small wind moves over me, as whispers reach me of a wretched and dirty man that the city should do something about, and I stare down at the dome and say goodbye again and again and again...

Chapter Eight

I find it in the usual spot.

Angie's RV is hard to miss. It's also a godsend for people like me. At present, there is no one around it, or seemingly inside. But I know she is, watching. She is always watching. Sometimes I wonder if she really is an angel. The Lord works in mysterious ways, and this just might be one of them.

It's been a long walk from Pike's Place to Godfrey Park at Artist Row. To say that my ankle hurts would be an understatement. Searing hot shooting electrifying vomitous pain. The branch/staff is not as helpful as the shopping cart, and so I'd kept my eye out for one of those along the way, but didn't see an abandoned one.

My head... yes, my head is clearing.

The scattering is... lessening.

The fragmenting is... dispersing.

I'm thinking in complete sentences. Well, sometimes. Not always, not always, but more than even just this morning. More than I had in a long time. Years and years.

I wince, take in some air, the pain... ugh. So much pain in my ankle. My poor foot is so damaged. Too damaged to ever be fixed, surely. I thought only of coping. The shopping cart, where was the shopping cart? The alley, yes, the alley. Far from here. Why did I leave it behind? The shelter. Something about the shelter. They don't allow carts, of course. I left it near the shelter. I need it, need it. My home, my room. Please, God, let it still be there.

The branch is fine. The branch is silly. People stare at me, and I don't blame them, I look like some ancient wizard walking down the street. No, not walking. Limping, dragging. My ankle... no support.

'Gandolf' appears in my thoughts, and I don't know where the word or name came from nor why.

I pause across the street, leaning against a light pole, sucking air, fighting the pain. It had been a long walk. A man slides past me now and looks at my branch, then looks at me and laughs. He is wearing slacks and a button up. Hair slicked back. A leather satchel strapped around his shoulder.

I smile at his laughter and join in. But he shakes his head, scowls. Whatever moment we had is gone, and I remain smiling even as he hurries down the street, even as my ankle hurts worse than I ever remember it hurting, ever, ever, ever.

I suck in air, sweating in my dirty pants, my dirty shirt. I wear only one shoe... a nice thick sock is best for my injured foot. A shoe... well, they don't fit. Sometimes I wear nothing. Until recently, I wasn't entirely sure when I hurt my foot or why I hurt my foot or who hurt my foot.

Thoughts coming... clearer.

Since when? Since the park of course. Since the girl with the missing tooth.

Not the first time. No, not the first time I had seen such a missing tooth on such a victim.

I stand and lean and gasp, sweating and hurting and waiting. I do not want to plumb my mind too deeply. Not now. Maybe never. The craziness is in there. A lot of it. Jumbled, angry, terrible, nonsensical, implausible, inhumane, distant, and alien thoughts are all in there. Not the kind of thoughts I want to explore.

I know this.

I'm also aware of other flashes of clarity, over the years. Usually, something awakens me from my stupor, my bliss, from the abyss, something that shocks me into sudden aware-ness. This clarity helps me find shelter from the cold, to remove myself from dangerous people, or from a dangerous part of the town. And once the danger is gone, once I settle into my new environment, once I am fed and warm and safe, the nonsense returns, descending down over me like a crazy, comforting, terrible blanket, and I wrap myself in it and let myself go, and my mind does just that... it goes and goes and goes, so far gone that I can't find it again, or even know where to look.

Until something wakes me again.

Like yesterday, when I found the body.

And the missing tooth. No, I did not find a missing tooth; I correct myself. I saw the gap in her bloodied mouth, where the tooth had been.

He's back, he's back, it's him, it's him.

I shake my head, getting a hold of my thoughts. I do not want them to get too jumbled. When they get jumbled, they sometimes stay jumbled. Clarity. Peace. Relax. Calm. Good, good.

He's back. The man who killed my daught-er.

It's him, him, him!

A growl escapes my mouth.

A man coming in my direction gives me a wide berth. I don't blame him. A growling homeless man is never something anyone wants to come across. I remind myself again that I'm around others. I remind myself again to actually care that I'm around others. In the past, I didn't care. In the past, I wasn't aware of the others. They were just noise. They were just moving parts. Some gave to me, most avoided me, others hurt me. Moving, living, loud, frightened obstacles.

No, I think now. They are living, breathing, good people.

Like me.

Like me.

Like me.

I take three deep, long, calming breaths. This is something I have always done. It is one of the few things I can rely on to relax me, even during the worst of the crazies. Three slow breaths later, I often had brief moments of clarity. I saw who I was, what I was, where I was, and I didn't like any of it. Surely this couldn't be me. Surely, I had jumped into the body of another. Surely I didn't live on the streets. Surely it was another who was dirty and sick and hungry and infested with bugs. I can feel them everywhere, even now. How I wasn't dead, I hadn't a clue, but there I stood, standing in any number of spots throughout the city, breathing deeply, awakened, and hating every second of it. The fog... the fog... the fog... The blessed fog where there is peace and insanity and oblivion...

Now I am awake and the fog doesn't seem so close. It's not far, no. I sense it, sense it.

But it is there and I am here.

I cross the street when it's safe to do so, knowing this hasn't always been the case for me. In the fog, I crossed streets randomly, without looking or caring or interested in my life or the lives of others. Cars slammed on brakes, fists were waved, drinks were thrown at me.

Safely across now, I struggle over the high curb, putting a lot of weight on my makeshift cane, and timing the hop of my good foot. There, there, just a slight stumble. Made it, made it.

Five minutes of shuffling, scraping, and groaning later, the RV looms before me, old, weathered, pealing, but big. I know inside lives an angel.

Thunderous footsteps behind me.

Someone accidentally kicks my branch, and it goes skittering over the sidewalk. Without it, I am left balancing on one leg, with only maybe ten or twenty percent of my body weight on my bad ankle. It can support some weight, enough that I don't tip over.

I hear myself apologizing, for obviously, I had stepped into the path of someone... or many someones. Perhaps joggers. The word sounds funny in my head. *Joggers*. Surely they are the source of all the running feet.

I feel terrible and wonder if someone had been hurt, perhaps even falling.

I stumble, searching for enough balance to turn around, to look around me, to take in what had happened. With pain radiating up for my foot, I keep from falling by spreading my arms out. A tight rope walker without the rope and without the pole. The mental image appeals to me, and I find myself smiling.

"Sorry," I hear myself saying aloud, and the word sounds crystal clear. I'm not stuttering as I usually do, seemingly incapable of forming sounds.

There are five of them, all young men, all wearing tank tops or t-shirts, all in jeans, except one, who wears cargo shorts. Two are smoking. Three look high. No, they all looked high. Correction, the one staring at me now, the twenty-something who shaved his eyebrows and wore his jeans low on his hips, with his boxer shorts spilling out like the top of a muffin, wasn't high. He stared at me with an unrelenting focus.

He seemed angry... and I know why.

I was supposed to fall, but I hadn't.

Not angry with me, I knew. After all, he had seen a hundred guys like me. No, these guys were only a few degrees separated from the street. Soon to be like me, and it scared the hell out of them. They hated themselves for it, and they hated me, and they hated the police, and their bosses and landlords and parents and ex-girlfriends and boyfriends and anyone else they saw as keeping them from having the fun they wanted to have... anyone who kept them from getting high or fucking or living.

And so the guy with the shaved eyebrows came at me... swinging something. A bottle. Not broken, but it would break if it landed where it was meant to land: my head. But I found my balance. I step back, hopping, and the bottle misses my temple, and as his arm continues forward, I instinctively swing a cupped hand down against his exposed ear. Not a punch, but a concussive explosion that surprises the hell out of him. He cries out, falls to a knee, holding his head. I would have cried out too. My blow had been perfectly timed for reasons I don't quite understand.

No, a distant memory of training... a memory that comes and goes...

Someone to my side picks up my walking stick. I am hopping now, putting almost no weight on my ankle, and so when the blow from the walking stick hits me, I am already a little off balance. I hop-skip to the right, certain I am about to fall over but I don't.

The guy swinging the stick loses his balance and spins to his knees. Most people, I know, don't know how to fight with such weapons. They swing too hard, over-exerting themselves, and this is knowledge I somehow know. I know, for instance, he would have been better off jabbing me with it, like a lance. But he didn't. Now, as he gets up from his skinned knees his jeans had holes in them already another comes at me from the other side. This one has something shining in his hand, a knife. My training—or whatever it was—had incorporated such attacks. I know I am no expert fighter either, and never was. Never really needed to be. I needed only to defend myself. But something within me knows what to do now, knows the motion I need to make.

I focus on the wrist and only the wrist, and as the knife swipes from left to right—perhaps he had intended to gut me—I catch his wrist in both my hands. I twist with all the strength I have. The knife falls and the kid cries out and now I lose my balance.

When I land, falling to my shoulder, I feel the first kick in my side, and then the second, and now someone stomps on my ear, crushing my head into the cement. The foot grinds into my face, harder and harder while other boots kick me and kick me and kick me... and I slip outside of myself... and float high above.

Chapter Nine

He is in pain. He is confused. He is lost.

He wonders where God has gone. He hates himself for wondering where God has gone.

He wonders if they will kill him. He wonders if he is dead now. He wishes he is dead.

The pain, the pain.

He thinks of his daughter. That someone like him had a daughter amazes him. He has gone years—a dozen or more years—without thinking of her.

He feels shut out of his own mind, his own body. The person lying on the ground is him but not him. The person on the ground wants it to end, wants these ruffians to finish him off, wants them to release him to God. And they are close, so close. He feels himself slipping, slipping.

The connection to this old and tired and abused husk is lessening...

He feels his mind expanding...

God, God, God...

Chapter Ten

A gunshot. It had to be a gunshot. I know the sound, although I don't hear it as often these days.

The weight on me is gone in a blink. I feel the blood flowing, and feel my nose moving under my skin, fragments of gristle against bone. My nose will need to be packed to heal properly. How I know this, I don't know.

The pool of liquid under my cheek is my own blood, not quite sticky yet, but would be soon. White halos and flashing light fill my head. I am certain I have a concussion, perhaps worse. I might have a cracked skull. I test my jaw there on the street. They did not break it. From my position on my side, I see the five young men back up. One is still holding my makeshift staff. He lifts it and breaks it over his knee. I notice other people keeping their distance. The guy with the tank top tosses the broken branches to the side and flips someone a double bird. One of the kids is bleeding from his ear. At least I had landed one blow.

Now a woman steps into view, standing in front of me, holding a pistol pointed at the sky. I hope a bullet didn't go through one of the surrounding skyscrapers. Now she points it at one of them and says she will shoot if they don't get. They don't want to be run off by an old woman, but the woman sounds like she means business, even if I can't entirely hear her, so loud is the buzzing in my head.

Finally, others join her, shouting for the young men to leave, and as they do so, I say a prayer of forgiveness for their hardened hearts, may they find the love of God, somewhere, anywhere. The old lady stands over me until I see the young men disappear around a corner. One of them shouts, bellowing into the sky, so charged he is with adrenaline. I pray most of all for him.

And when they are gone, the woman turns and looks down at me. I try to smile until I realize a tooth is embedded in my lower lip. I work it out and spit it to the side as she helps me sit up. I want to black out, but I am past that stage. After all, this isn't my first beating. Truth be known, I've endured worse.

"You need an ambulance, friend?" she asks, kneeling down on one knee. I can smell the sulfur wafting off her gun. I used to know that smell well.

Memories of me in a shooting range emerge from the depths. In it, I am young, serious, committed, skilled. I hold the gun with two hands, taking careful aim, enjoying the process of shooting more than I cared to admit.

I shake my head, and run my tongue along a deep cut inside my lower lip, where the tooth got embedded. I feel a strong hand grip me under my armpit. The effort helps pull me up to my hands and knees. I shake my head, clearing it, and watch briefly as blood drip-drips from my face.

"Come inside, friend. We're making a scene. Plus, I hear sirens."

A minute or two later, I shuffle up wobbly stairs and into the RV, just as a police cruiser, sirens wailing, moves past the curtained windows. Its strobing lights paint the walls behind me. It doesn't slow, likely because it's not sure what to look for, and by the time I climbed the stairs the crowd had mostly dispersed.

The RV isn't like other RVs. My memory of it is vague, having been inside it at least once before. Somewhere in the fog, I had made my way here, perhaps maybe even a few times. Once inside, she guided me to a familiar chair: a barber's chair, in fact. Overhead, wires and CVC piping criss-crossed the RV's interior, from which hung hundreds of pieces of clothing: jackets and sweaters and pants and long underwear and thermal long sleeves and t-shirts. So many t-shirts. The jackets numbered nearly as many... or maybe they only looked that way because of their bulk.

The place seems smaller to me now. My memory of it was something cavernous, endless. Then again, I'd been in the fog and there's no trusting those memories. Amazing that I have any memories of it at all. God only knows what I have forgotten, but that's okay. Most memories should stay forgotten. Nobody should be encumbered with the nightmares I have mostly forgotten.

My face hurts. All of it, from my earlobes to my eyebrows. It hurts when I blink and it hurts when I don't blink. Everything hurts, throbs, and I groaned when the nice woman hands me a few gelcap painkillers. I don't take drugs, but I take these, because the pain in my head seems to be growing and I am wondering again if I have a fractured skull.

I feel myself wanting to slip into the fog, the pain is so great. There is no pain in there, there is only light and darkness and confusion and peace.

"Hey, you still there?" asks a voice in front of me.

I nod my head, not trusting words yet. I haven't trusted words in God knows how long.

Twenty years, roughly. Maybe more, maybe less.

"Good. Did you swallow the Advil?"

I nod, opening my mouth, searching with my tongue. Wait. There they are. Oops. I make to hold up a finger and am surprised to see that I'm holding a glass of water. I take a sip and swallow the pills with the water. I hope the painkillers work fast. Maybe they will. My stomach is empty. Pills should absorb. I know this somehow.

I know this.

I know lots of things. I know a lifetime of things.

So many things. There, inside me. Waiting, waiting.

"Hey, snap out of it. Your eyes are going all... crazy. Like how you used to look back in the day."

My eyebrows go up, perhaps quizzically, a

painful gesture that I won't make again anytime soon.

"Yes, I remember you. The broken ankle. How could I forget? You're one of the ones I think of most. Glad to see you. Sorry about the shitheads. They don't know how close they were to being popped. Had one lined up, too, but decided to shoot in the air instead. Why they beat you up? Why not beat up the asshole double-parked next door?"

I don't make a sound or move, although I follow her with my eyes. Her eyes follow my eyes.

"You got one of them, didn't you? Saw it as I was coming down the stairs. Sorry, would have been here earlier, but I had to get the gun, you know?"

I want to nod but I don't. The pain, the pain...

"Hey, stay with me, fella. Don't drift off. Not yet. And not that way. Sleep is fine, not that vacant, deer in the headlights, crazy ass shit. You get that look and I know there's no reaching you... or any of them. Good, good, there you are. Do you recognize me?"

She is small and stocky, with a lot of skin hanging from her upper arms. She wears a floral dress with white socks and white canvas shoes. She is clean and neat and smells nice. The pills haven't kicked in yet, but I risk nodding. She is as I remember, though tougher than I remember. Then again, I only see her in the hazy mist of my memory, barely there. But it is her, it is her. The nodding hurts, but not quite as bad as I feared. Still, the movement hurts my teeth.

"Hey. Good, glad you remember me. You come here to get cleaned up?"

I'm still reeling from the nod and have to wait before I can answer.

"Give it a few more minutes, fella. You'll start feeling a little better. Meanwhile, I'm gonna go look for your size."

By the time she returns with folded jeans, a black t-shirt, socks, boxers and a nice pair of used Nike sneakers, I ask if she would mind terribly if I replaced the jeans for some slacks, and the t-shirt for a button down short-sleeved shirt. She looks me over, nods. "You looking for work?"

"I'm looking for something." My voice sounds strange, distant, old, weak, deep and not my own. It also might have squeaked, so rarely do I use it.

"He speaks! I ain't never heard you speak before. Thought maybe you couldn't."

"I can speak," I say.

"Good to know. If not for work, whatcha looking for?"

"Someone."

"And you need to dress fancy-like?"

"I think so, yes..." I search for the phrasing, for the sentence construction, for the thought I wish to convey. "I might need to get into places I might not otherwise get into."

"What kind of places?"

I think about that. "Police stations, businesses, housing tracks. I don't know yet."

"Are you looking for the person who did this." She points to my twisted ankle.

"No."

"Who then?"

I say nothing. My head is slowly spinning. This isn't the fog. This is worse. This is, I think, a seizure of some sort. The spinning turns to a staticy crackle, but I know how to stop it.

I hum to myself. The humming turns into a song that I mostly make up, though I am pretty sure it's a 70's disco classic. I hum and rock and the spinning slows, slows. I sing some more, a little louder, my eyes open and focus on my good foot and its torn shoe. The spinning stops and I close my eyes and feel the tears on my cheeks. Not sure where the tears came from or why, but I am surprised to see the woman holding both my hands.

"You okay, fella?"

"Yes."

"It's not so bad, you know."

"What's not so bad?"

"Life, living. With a little luck, you can be okay."

"Thank you."

"I found you some nicer clothing. Should fit."

"Thank you."

"You're looking for the person who did this." She makes a general gesture toward me. "The person who stole your life?"

I nod, and keep nodding as she goes back to squeezing my hands.

"C'mon, fella. Let's get you cleaned up so that you can find this son of a bitch."

Chapter Eleven

I showered first. Long and hard.

Dirt caked every crease and fold of my body. I scrubbed furiously. Leaves and twigs emerged from my head and beard. In one instance, something that looked very much like a dead cockroach dropped to the shower floor. My time was limited in her shower. She had, I knew, only so much water. Already it grew cold. Truthfully, cold showers didn't bother me. Try as I might, I really couldn't remember my last hot shower. Probably at the shelter, with other men, in a big, open stall filled with a rat's nest of foul hair and a steady stream of filthy water swirling into the center drain. The water, at times, had been so brown I couldn't see my feet.

I shake my head now, and my longish hair shakes with it. Enough with the tangled, filthy hair. If I'm going to find this son of a bitch, I had to be presentable—at least, as presentable as I could.

The shower stall is narrow, and I lean against the malleable walls, taking weight off my broken ankle. Technically, it wasn't still broken. It had been broken... and then neglected. It had needed to be set and it hadn't been. I cleaned my ears and could hardly believe how much mud and coagulated blood dropped out. I cleaned around and around my ears, too, watching as less and less filth dropped free. I cleaned in other places, places so foul and rotten and caked with rot that I spent the remainder of my time in that shower apologizing to anyone who ever had the misfortune to sit, stand, or be upwind of me.

By the time I finished, the shower had grown ice cold, and the water swirling down the drain looked clean enough.

I was exhausted.

***

The haircut and beard trim came next.

If she was turned off, repulsed, or squeamish by what she found in my head or beard, she didn't show it. I knew I had a cut on my head from somewhere recently. Not the teen punks, something else, a fall, I think. I knew also that a skin condition presently affected my jawline. I knew my skin itched there, more so than anywhere else on my body. Sometimes I scratched until I bled.

She carefully sheared around the damaged skin on my face. When the hair had been removed, she studied the wounds at my jaw, her eyes wide and concerned behind her bifocals. With a steady stream of pedestrians passing just beyond the partially opened rear side window of the RV, she gently applied an ointment to my skin. I think the ointment was part Neosporin and part cannabis oil, which goes by an acronym that I don't remember. Then again, I am impressed that the words Neosporin, cannabis and acronym have formed in my mind. I often struggle over words for hours... until I forget what word I struggled to find. To see the words appear now, easily in my mind, is enough to make me smile.

"What are you smiling about?" she asks, still applying the ointment.

"I'm remembering."

"What are you remembering?"

"Words. Big words, too."

"I'm happy for you, fella. Words will help you find this guy. What did he do anyway?"

I can't find it within myself to say, try as I might. I feel my jaw quivering with the effort, but I am afraid to say it, afraid of what it might do to me, afraid to feel broken and helpless all over again.

"It's okay, fella. He's a bad man. We can leave it at that."

I nod, but still feel my jaw quivering, and the big words I had remembered are gone again, and for the life of me, I can't remember them now... ointment? Was that one of the words? Maybe, maybe. I don't know; I don't know.

And now I find myself crying, and this strange woman holding my head lightly, pressing her forehead against mine and telling me I'm going to be okay and that she is sorry and she wants me to know I am loved by her and by God, and I smile and stop crying and settle down, and feel myself drifting to sleep, as her fingers move through my hair, and the sound of the scissors reminds me of the hiss of a snake...

Chapter Twelve

I am standing in front of a mirror, dressed to the nines, or maybe eights, since I am missing a shoe.

I wear one black sneaker that might be new. Whether it is new or not does not matter to me. That it fits doesn't matter. What it represents... matters a little more. I am trying to be presentable. I am trying to be taken seriously. I am trying to find answers. People don't talk to people like me. I need to change that. I need to look... normal. I need to sound normal, too.

My other foot is bedecked in a thick black sock that should hold up a few days before holes appear in them, along the outside of my foot, of course, where it drags a little behind me.

Who I expect to talk to, I don't know. What I will say to them, I don't know that either.

But I do know this... whatever I am about to do, I am good at it.

I know this because that's who I was in 'those days,' even if 'those days' feel stranger than hell to me.

'These days' and 'those days.' That's how I've come to think of the time before my time spent on the streets. My life in two parts. The first when I was *him*. The second when I am *me*. The thing is... as my head clears, as the memories return, I think of him more and more and me less and less. I think of the man he was, the life he had, and I am curious, thrilled. Mercifully, only a few memories filter through. Not too many. Too many would be too much. I can barely handle what I remember now, for many of them are filled with unbearable sadness. Mostly, I see the little girl, the sweet angel he loved with all his heart. The memories of her growing, growing, growing, and becoming such a beautiful young lady. Oh, the sweet memories. But woven through all of them is terrible anguish, too, so much so that I have to stop thinking about them. It is then that I often forget who I am all over again, and find myself weeping for no good reason.

There is another woman in *his* memories, a beautiful mature perfect lovely glorious woman who makes his heart thump when he thinks of her. I feel what the man feels. I feel his love for her, although I do not remember her. No, wait. Yes, I do. No, I don't. Yes, I do. She is the one, the one, the one. Where is she? He doesn't know, and neither do I.

My head feels so scrambled at these memories, as I remember more and more of them, as these images and thoughts and feelings return. Who is she? Who is the little girl all grown up, the little one who breaks his heart so?

In rare moments of clarity, I know exactly who she is. I know exactly who both of them are.

The rare moments of clarity, so far, don't stick. They come and go and I find myself weeping.

Stick, dammit. Who are you, who are you, who are you?

I love them; I know. I love them and they loved me.

I feel the woman's eyes on me in the RV. She is sitting on a small cushioned bench behind a small fold-out table. She had already swept my hair off the floor. I had reached down to help and she caught me before I fell. She said it was okay. She had cleaned up plenty of hair in her time and knew just how to do it. She had added the words with a wink, and a pat on my now smooth face, where the ointment cooled my jaw. My eyes and lips felt puffy from the beating earlier, but I paid them no mind.

The man in the mirror is tallish and bent slightly to the right, like a "C." He looks like he is compensating for a broken ankle, which of course he is. This makes me smile, and man in the mirror smiles too. I can see the wounds on his hairline and eyes and lips, the gleam of ointment on his jaw, the way his right foot curls under him, the grotesqueness of the injury hidden within the thick sock. Had the sock not been there, the foot would make most people squeamish. It made me squeamish, too.

"You look handsome, friend."

"Thank you," I say, but the words don't really compute, not at the moment. The man in the mirror is me? I do not recognize him. I do not know him. Quite frankly, it is freaking me out that he stares at me so. What happened to his face? He took a beating, surely. And his ankle. His poor ankle...

My head spins. I close my eyes, brace myself.

I know the man is me. I know it, but I don't know it. I want to believe, and maybe I do believe.

No. Not me, not me, not me.

No, no, no.

"You okay, fella?"

"I... I don't know."

"Well, you look okay. In fact, you even look handsome."

I say nothing. Handsome. I know the word. I haven't heard it in a very long time. Years and years. It is a lost word. The lost words are coming back to me more and more. I do not remember the lost words until I need them. Sometimes they wait for me to find them. Sometimes I never find them, and it's frustrating. Mostly I don't care. Sometimes the words come to me later, and I forget why I needed them, but there they are. Foolproof came to me earlier today. Why, I don't know. But there it was in my thoughts.

Foolproof. I say it again, and again. I am not exactly sure what it means. It sounds so... off to my ear. I like it but don't like it. God says to never call another man a fool. So why have proof of a fool? Or does it mean something else? I don't know. I don't know.

"Settle down, fella. It's okay. What's got you worked up?"

"Foolproof."

"I see. Okay, on second thought I don't see at all."

"What does it mean?"

"It means... hmm. Anyone can do it. No one can mess it up. Why do you want to know?"

I say nothing.

She comes up behind me and puts a hand on my shoulder. "Words are hard to remember, I know."

I say nothing.

"Don't let it get you down, fella. You'll remember some words and forget others. Just find the easiest word for now. The bigger ones can come later."

Her own words are what I need to hear, and I let the word go. Foolproof. Yes, it means easy, I think. Easy, easy. Anyone can do it, even a fool.

"You haven't been called handsome in a long time, I take it."

I say nothing. I'm not sure what to say. She seems to know my thoughts. Then again, maybe my thoughts aren't so hard to know. Then again, maybe I am speaking my thoughts. I do that sometimes.

"You almost forgot the word."

I want to nod, but don't.

"It's the first compliment you've heard in a long time, and you don't know how to react, or even to believe it."

I say nothing, hands holdings hands.

"Well, you are. I'm sure you've seen better days, and you could gain a few pounds, too, but you are a handsome man. Do you have any money? Of course you don't. Here."

She steps around me, between myself and the mirror, and hands me a $20 bill. It is a sight that warms me from the inside. I haven't held a $20 bill in a long time. Maybe never in my second life. My first life... yes, I'm sure of it. Who was I?

The word detective appears in my thoughts. I am not quite sure I remember what it means.

But I know it is me.

Detective.

She pushes the money into my hand. "Take it, fella. Buy a hot meal. Anyone will serve you now. You can go anywhere looking like this. Anywhere. You clean up well. How's your face?"

I say nothing.

"Well, I'm sure it hurts. I'm sorry they hurt you. I saw you fight back. Boy, you fought back. If it wasn't for your foot... and so many of them... I don't think they would have taken you. Where did you learn to fight like that?"

"I was a detective, once," I hear myself saying, and the strength in my voice surprises me.

"Were you now?"

"It was a long time ago."

"Imagine that. A police detective?"

"Yes."

"That might explain it. Who are you after?"

"My daughter." The word sounds so foreign and harsh to my ear, that I recoil at it.

"Settle down, fella. Relax. Breathe. We're just talking here. No one will hurt you. You are looking for your daughter?"

I shake my head once, take in some air. The panic passes, and I feel... stronger.

"Someone... hurt your daughter?"

I nod, say nothing, take another breath, ball my fists. The twenty dollar bill is in the left one, crumpled now.

"I'm sorry, fella I hope she is okay. She's not okay, is she? Shit, I'm sorry."

"It's okay," I say, and I like the strength in my voice.

"Did someone kill her?"

For the first time, I look her in the eye and nod once.

"How long ago?"

I don't know how long ago. But I say nothing.

"A long time ago?" she says.

I nod.

"And somehow you ended up here, on the streets."

I nod, say nothing.

"Where you lost yourself and forgot about her. But here you are now, remembering. Remembering her and remembering words all over again. Why now?"

I say nothing at first. Then open my mouth to speak. "He's back."

"The killer?"

I nod.

"And you know this how?"

She will not understand how I know. But she surprises me.

"The girl in the woods, last week?"

"Yes."

"You're sure?"

"Yes."

"Hold on."

She disappears in the back of the RV and returns with two things. She hands me a small revolver first. "There's a single shot in there. It's one of those lady guns from nearly a century ago. Last I heard it works. Can't go chasing a killer without a gun, can you?"

I stare at it... and take it gently. I slip it in my pocket.

Next, she hands me one more thing. Well, two more things.

_THE PALE COLD LIGHT

Chapter Thirteen

The crutches take some getting used to.

At first, I couldn't remember their name, but as I tested them out in the RV, it came to me. Crutches, everyone knows crutches.

Now, I move along the sidewalk with no weight on my bad ankle. Most importantly, there's no pain. Well, maybe a little. The ankle, after all, always hurts. But the shooting pain that brought tears to my eyes is gone.

A few blocks later, I finally get the hang of it.

Once, a woman said she would return with some crutches. I waited three days; she never returned. Walking canes are okay but only absorb about half of my weight. Same with shopping carts, though sometimes I hopped along on my good foot, holding my bad one up. I would do that until I grew tired and stopped and sat by the shopping cart. Sometimes the shopping cart got away from me as I leaned on it and skipped on one good foot. Once or twice I fell. Once or twice I fell into the cart, too, tipping it over, tipping all my stuff onto me and across the sidewalk.

Usually I just put some of my weight on the cart, not all of it, and walked carefully on my bad ankle, despite the terrible pain. Sometimes I didn't have a shopping cart and had to make do. Years ago, I used an old rake I'd found leaning against a tree. I walked the side streets of Seattle like that, knowing people looked at me oddly, knowing people talked about me. Very few helped me up curbs. Some gave me money and half-eaten hamburgers. Most turned their eyes away from me. This is all a blur. These are scattered, incoherent memories. Endless streets, endless parks, endless curbs and park benches and trees and blankets and shelters. Years lost, memories lost, words lost, mind lost. But I got through it, didn't I?

More than anything, I feel as if I am emerging from a dream. A long, long, long dream. But I've felt this awakening before, though it didn't stick. Flashes of clarity that lasted minutes, sometimes hours, only to fade, swallowed whole in the fog.

But this clarity has been going on for days now. The missing tooth had been the trigger. I'm sure of it. After all, I had seen another girl missing a tooth. The same front tooth in fact. My girl, my girl, my girl.

Memories returning. Words returning. Life returning. Strength returning. Resolve returning. Pain returning. All of it returning.

No, not all. I do not want it all. Some can stay forgotten.

Some memories are so scattered that I will never make sense of them, and that is okay. I need only know that I made it from that point, to this point. And this is the point I need to be. Right here, right now. All that other stuff got me here. It served a purpose. The craziness, the hunger, the pain, the lost memories. I'm still here, right where I need to be.

My mind is damaged. I can sense that. There is a hole there that I can almost see. I sense it, surely. It's there in my thoughts. I need only to step back and drop in and disappear for a while. Sometimes it's good to disappear and forget and huddle and weep and talk and talk and talk, even if I do not know what I am saying.

The hole is there. I sense it. I need only to

step back into it if I want to.

But I do not want to step back.

Not now. I want to move forward.

It's time, it's time.

He's here, here, here.

Somewhere nearby.

I need my wits about me. I need my mind. I need my strength. I need my legs. I need this gun with the single bullet. I need clear thoughts. I need access to words. I need to communicate and work with others. I need to investigate this like I know I can. I need to look and act normal.

I need... I need... I need...

I need to find the fucker. He eluded me back in the day. He eluded us all. He killed and disappeared. But he's here now and he's killing again, and he's taking his trophies, one of which was my daughter's tooth. Her front tooth.

Sick piece of shit.

Focus. Keep it together. Plug the hole.

And find this fucker.

Forgive me, Father.

I take in some air, shake my head. I'm getting used to the crutches, getting used to holding my bad ankle up, to moving forward again.

Far, far, far away from the hole.

Chapter Fourteen

The sun is brighter and I have to shield my eyes but the crutches are occupying my hands. A ball-cap. I'll have to see if my friend in the RV has an extra ball-cap next time.

Was it always so bright? It's like a curtain has been opened. Or a rock has been lifted. That's it. The rock I'd kept myself under isn't there any longer, so the sun is brighter. I know if I keep looking into the sun I will blind myself, so I look away now, but I'm still seeing a bright yellow orb with shooting stars everywhere.

What was her name? The one in the park who I found near my dog's grave. Her name reminds me of another dog, one I remember from when I was young. I want to say Shaggy. Shaggy is not the name of the girl *or* the dog.

I step into the next alley and stand in the shadows. My eyes are slowly returning to normal. I rub them, trying to erase the sun's ghost from my vision.

Daphne. The girl's name was Daphne. And she was kind to me. I would see her in the park on the bench where I liked to sit or sleep. It was a favorite of mine, near a drinking fountain, near a bathroom. It had a feeling of being at home. I'd always be disappointed when I returned to the bench and found someone on it. I couldn't tell them they didn't belong there. It wasn't mine. But it was my home. Sometimes.

The first time I met Daphne was on that bench. She had invited me to sit with her. Few invited me to sit with them. She shared a sandwich with me. It was toasted bread and had lettuce and carefully folded pieces of meat. *Ham and cheese*. It was the best food I ever tasted in all the time under the rock. And she said I could share her sandwich whenever I saw her in the park.

And so I did. I shared many sandwiches with her in that park, often on that bench. A favorite of hers was... I don't remember; I don't remember. A city, a city. I shake my head now. Philly. It was a Philly, and it was very warm and gooey and wonderful. That was the best food I'd ever tasted in all the time under the rock. Or, no, there was the time she brought a couple white boxes of Chinese food. The food was fried rice with bits of egg and peas and little cut carrots and beef. And *it* was the best food I ever had under the rock. And one of those white boxes of Chinese food she had brought *just for me*.

I think about how I must've looked to her. My dirty long beard and hair, with leaves and probably a twig or two. My coat with rips and dried blood and mud. My foot twisted and unnaturally lumpy. And my eyes not able to make contact with hers for very long at all. Being under the rock—or in the hole— meant I didn't occupy the same world as everybody else. So my eyes got used to seeing the world and other people without looking directly at them.

And she didn't care. Didn't judge. She just smiled.

And that killer. He took her life, too. He took so much away from me. He's the one who sent me under the rock in the first place.

The piece of shit.

I know cussing is wrong, but I also know God will forgive me.

And now the rock is gone. I'm walking

under the same sun as everyone else. I'm taking the same risks as everyone else. I'm going to look into the eyes of the people I talk to and I'm going to find the killer who took Daphne away from the world.

Daphne and my daughter.

And I know where to start, too.

Chapter Fifteen

The park with the bench is near the red-light district.

Red-light district. That's a term I haven't used in years. That's because it's a term left over from my earlier life. Before my years under the rock. But the language I used from that earlier life is like a muscle that's rusty but still working, phrases and terms I can remember when I worked these neighborhoods as a police detective. I thought I knew these streets back then, as I went about processing crime scenes and following hunches and ferreting out the bad eggs from the merely troubled.

But nobody knows the streets like those who live on them. My knowledge and under-

standing of these areas has grown exponentially. *Exponentially*. I'm a walking thesaurus. I
would wager there aren't five homeless in this
whole city who walk around using the word
exponentially.

So, I'm heading to the red-light district, a
street corner off the beaten path where women
like Daphne could stand and be noticed by
johns looking for some affection. Police don't
harass the business that's conducted on the
street corner in the red-light district because it's
not happening in plain sight of polite society.
As long as they keep their business in the
shadows, then the police won't go prowling
those shadows. I hate to use the term win-win,
but there you go.

I haven't used the term win-win since my
earlier life. That's because life under the rock
never had a situation that could be described as
a win-win. Generally, situations were lose-lose
or lose-death.

It is later and I have walked many miles
with the crutches and my arms are shaking and
my smooth face is getting sunburned. The rough
skin at my jawline is drying out. Healing, I
think.

The red-light district.

The women standing on the corner are like
Daphne: attractive but beaten down. They try to

portray themselves as the ones in control of the situation, but any time they drive away with someone they've lost all control. So they wear their miniskirts and tight corsets and halter tops, and they flaunt their bodies and give winks and come-hither smiles. But they're never in control and they're just one car-ride away from the same fate as Daphne.

I choose a pair of women that I can recall Daphne being friendly with. They're both black. One is very tall and wears a tight red vinyl mini-dress. She has a giant mane of golden hair and cheekbones that make her face triangular. The other one is short and very heavy. Her butt is falling out of her black leather short-shorts and her bosom is overflowing her bra. That's all she's wearing. She looks like a cake pan of overflowing flesh.

"Hey, handsome, what're you interested in today?" the taller one asks. Her voice is deep. I notice her Adam's Apple.

I search for words, try out a few, struggle, struggle.

"It's okay, handsome. I have that effect on people." She laughs and touches my shoulder.

I try again, and again, and again, and almost weep, but don't. She keeps her hand on my shoulder, reassuringly. An angel, this one. Well, a kind of angel.

I try again and find the words. "I'm... I'm trying to find somebody who could tell me about Daphne."

The taller one removes her hand and crosses them over her chest. Her face scrunches. She is confused. "What do you want with Daphne?"

"I'm... I'm trying to find who... who killed her." I'd debated whether or not to be straight-forward. My experience from my earlier life taught me that not everybody should be questioned in the same manner. Some needed to dance a bit beforehand, foreplay I called it. But some, like these two women on the street corner, didn't have time to waste with me. So straightforward it was.

The taller one is contemplative. She knows something. The short one laughs, mean and contemptuous.

"What're you going to do, Superman? Chase the guy down with your crutches and bore him to death?" She rolls her eyes.

"You said 'the guy.'"

"Go away, Superman. You're interrupting our lives."

I turn to the taller one. "Do you know who it was? Do you know who killed Daphne?"

She twists a finger in her golden mane. "I don't know. But I keep my ears open."

"Did the police ever question anybody around here?"

The short one laughs humorlessly. "Please, don't any police come around asking us about dead girls. They couldn't care less about us." She bends over as a car pulls tight to the curb and jiggles her boobs. She's jiggling all over. It's not a pretty sight. The driver must agree because he moves off. "See that, Superman? You're killing our traffic."

"So, the police never questioned anybody?"

"Nope," says the angry one. "One more dead street girl is one less thing they have to worry about."

Not true, not true. We cared about each case. I know this; I remember this, even if the details are fuzzy. Some cases are more likely to be solved than others. We cared—I cared—it's just that some cases had leads, others didn't. We need clues to solve cases, suspects. Something, anything.

"Why's he shaking his head?" asks the little one.

"I don't know."

"Lookin' like he's gonna cry."

I pull it together. I need to know what the tall one knows. Dead street girls. I'd seen my fair share back in the day. Bad memories, bad memories. The little one... maybe she has a point. I remember stamping files—too many files—"Open and Active" and shoving them into the big black filing cabinet we called the Black Hole. We cared, I cared. No leads, nothing. What were we supposed to do? Cases piled up.

I take a breath, calm myself. "I'm interested, I'm interested and I'm asking questions." I hold my chin up and make eye contact with the tall one. The short one is probably thinking more rude and obnoxious things and so I ignore her. "Do you know who might have hurt Daphne?"

"Hurt? Try killed, asshole."

I ignore the angry one some more.

The tall one shrugs, keeping eye contact. "Daphne was smart. She was sweet but cautious. I don't think she would've put herself into a situation that she couldn't get herself out of."

I nodded, caught the subtext. I don't think I've caught subtext in two decades, but I caught it here. "This wasn't a regular, ah, business transaction? Perhaps someone new?"

The angry one snorts. "Transaction? What are you? A stock market guy? Did you trip on your way to the top and break your damn foot?" She laughs and her boobs jiggle.

I look away from the jiggling boobs.

I shake my head. I feel dizzy, uneasy. This

isn't me... talking to two strangers like I mean it.

No, this is me. This used to be me. I used to be good at this. Damn good at this.

Breathe, breathe, relax, relax, good, good.

The tall one has seen something, but doesn't know enough to come clean. I got what I want. Verify, verify.

"A stranger, then," I say, glancing at the tall one, who nods imperceptively.

"Please be smart and stay safe. No strangers."

"Okay, whatever."

"I'll be around." I begin backing away on my crutches. "If somebody asks about Daphne, get their name."

"Okay, bye-bye." The short one gives me a dismissive wave.

"What's your name?" the tall one asks.

"You already know it." I pause and turn. They're both confused. "I'm Superman."

Chapter Sixteen

A block away, I sit inside a McDonald's, sipping a hot coffee with a little sugar and cream, trying to remember her.

No, not Daphne. But *her.* I can't see her face or remember her name. Daphne keeps coming to mind. So similar, so similar. I shake my hands and shake my head, frustrated. She's in there, in there. Lord, help me remember.

I built castle walls to keep certain doors shut, to keep certain invaders safely outside. But those same castle walls also kept things bottled up inside. They're the reason I'm walking on crutches. My ankle was crushed and the castle walls kept me from finding medical help. And the ankle would always serve as a reminder: go back inside those walls at your own peril. Nothing penetrates the walls, good or bad. You're just stuck inside with yourself.

It is late afternoon when I exit McDonald's. I'm down to $19.31. Coffee is still cheap. Go figure.

There is a construction site nearby and I gravitate toward it. Here, the sidewalk has been covered by scaffolding and wood-plank ceiling, leaving a tunnel to walk through. I'm still only a block from the girls working the street corner. I guess you could say I'm red-light district adjacent. Something told me to stick around this area, so I stuck around.

The covered sidewalk is dark and the two blinking halogen lights don't offer much illumination. I tread carefully in the gloom, worried that my crutches might find a crack or slant that could drop me to the pavement.

I get beyond the tunnel and gaze skyward at the building that's going up. It's almost ten stories high with no end in sight. The tall crane that's hoisting up an I-beam is at least double the unfinished structure's height. Although the construction site has a barrier wall that obstructs my view of its ground level, I have no problem seeing the rest of the project.

Several welders are working aloft, melding sections of steel with their arcs of white fire, creating yellow starbursts of sparks that flick against their face-shields and rain down across the worksite.

Some of the welders take a pause, facing toward the street corner I just left. I can't see what's drawn their attention so I double-back through the tunnel of scaffolding. When I reach fading daylight, I spot the object of their adulation: a new female is working the nearby red-light district. She's tall and blonde, wearing a white catsuit that shows off every statuesque curve. She's like the old Corvette Stingrays I used to covet: not a straight line on her.

I smile not at the imagery, but at the memory. The recall had been almost instant.

Wow, wow, wow. I'm back.

I'm back.

Back.

Sort of. Not really. Some memories pour through, some struggle through. Still, not bad, not bad. I would take this keen memory. This fun memory.

I pause, close my eyes, and let my mind peek inside another door that's long been sealed: my prowess as a detective. When I was working homicide I used to joke with the guys that I had a sort of Spidey Sense. An intuition. It would manifest itself as a prickling along my scalp, as if the clues in front of my face were knocking on my cranium to get my attention.

What am I seeing here? Why am I getting the pricking sensation *right now*?

The construction site is only a block from where Daphne used to work, and maybe a mile from the park where she was found dead. She was killed—as far as my fog-addled brain can figure—less than a week ago. This construction site has been around for at least four months. I'm basing my estimate on the progress they've made, not by consulting my fuzzy memory banks. Until now I haven't even noticed this place. Sure, I've probably passed it a thousand times but that was when I was still under the rock, inside my castle walls, in the deep hole.

So, if the excitable welders are any indication, and the working girls that they're ogling are only a block away, then this construction site offers up a tantalizing amount of possibilities. I could very well be looking at the spot where Daphne's demise was hatched.

The killer could be here, right in front of my face, knocking on my skull.

Chapter Seventeen

I weigh my options.

I could just sit on the bench at the bus stop across the street. Just sit back and monitor the situation. Keep my eyes peeled for any activity between the construction guys and those girls on the street corner. But that would be risky.

Only a street person parks himself on a bench for hours at a time. I'm no longer a street person, right? I'm wearing ordinary clothes and have a fresh-shaved face and clean hair. People don't see me as a street person. Part of me misses that obscurity, that sense of being invisible to anyone and everyone; in this case, the freedom to perform a stakeout in plain sight.

So, although the bench would offer me the

most advantageous view, I just can't afford the exposure. I need to find something else.

A bit of a ways down the block is a diner called Finley's. It's further away than the bus stop, and its shopfront window doesn't have a great view of the street corner I'm trying to watch. But it's all I have to work with at the moment. If I play my cards right, and don't overdo it, I might be able to move between the diner and the bus stop bench.

Minutes later, I ease into Finley's and breathe in the warm heaven of a skillet at work. Eggs, burgers, bacon... it's a symphony of scents that makes my eyes and mouth water, unlocking smells and memories of a home life that I'd kept far outside the castle walls. Mc Donald's smelled good, but it hadn't unlocked the vault.

A portly guy with a hairnet is at the grill. He waves his spatula.

"Welcome to Finley's! Savannah is getting some stuff from the fridge so just seat yourself."

I blink, wondering who he's speaking to at first—me, me, me—and take a seat in a corner booth. The best seat in the house for my purposes, right near the window.

I touch the $19 and change in my pants pocket, the bills folded neatly in half. They give me a feeling of legitimacy. A sense of worth. I open the menu. The prices are all in the $5.00 range. Now if I can just slow-play my time and my money...

"Hey, there, Sugar," says Savannah, the waitress. She's older and wrinkled, but wrinkled in all the right places: Along the mouth and eyes, where frequent smiles leave their trace. She reacts to my face, her mouth lines shifting down into a frown. "My word, did you get the license plate of the truck that hit you?"

I realize she's waiting for a response but two decades without chit-chat has left such skills a little rusty.

I finally think of a response: "An L, I think."

"Come again?" Her pencil is poised over her small order pad.

"The truck's license plate. I believe it started with an L." I try to smile so she knows I'm attempting chit-chat and not really conveying information about the imaginary truck. My face hurts from the smile because the bruises along cheekbones are all puckering. The skin at my jaw is still raw.

"Oh, that's good, Sugar. Maybe by dessert will have the whole number." She waves her pencil over the notepad. "Whatcha want?"

I open the menu and squint at the prices, finding the lowest full meal. "Three-dollar-and-thirty cents."

"So far so good. But like the L, I need more information."

Oh, shit. I said the words out loud. Meant to think them. No reason to explain, so I power through. "Um, I meant the pancakes and bacon breakfast."

"A breakfast for dinner man. Juice or coffee?"

I check the menu prices, squinting, not sure if I'm saying the prices out loud again, hoping I'm not.

"Juice," she decides for me. "And the coffee's on me." She winks and heads back behind the counter.

Had I said the prices out loud? Is that why the coffee was on her? I didn't know, I didn't know, and now my head slowly spins, slowly, slowly. I run my fingers through my hair, pull on the follicles hard enough that I wince. Then I pat my hair down, breathe, breathe. All is well.

I check out the window. From where I sit, I can see that the welders are back at work on the upper floors, sparks flying. Six welders. To the right, I count three high steel workers guiding the I-beam into place. A half dozen more guys with hardhats are in the upper reaches of the skeletal building but they're too far overhead to get an exact number.

So what made my Spidey Sense go off? Just because some guys took a work-break to eyeball a beautiful woman? Well, not just any woman. A working woman. A hooker. But no, that's not enough to raise a red flag, to speculate that a killer might be behind, say, one of those welding torches.

The waitress is back with my juice. She fills my coffee cup from her carafe.

"How long has that building been going up?" I hear myself ask, my voice soft and distant.

"Months. I want them to take as long as possible. Because once they get to finishing the damn thing, the sun is going bye-bye."

"Total eclipse?"

"Maybe some rays here or there, but nothing you can get a tan by. We can kiss half the day goodbye, sitting in its damn shadow."

I make sympathetic noises. I think.

"Oh," I say suddenly. "I thought of another letter: A."

"Are we back on the license plate?"

I nod and take a sip of coffee.

"You got a quirky sense of humor, Sugar." She winks again and moves on to the next booth.

The time is four o'clock. Almost knock-off time. I can picture the cartoon with the caveman... Fred Flintstone. Didn't he work construction? All I can recall is that the bell they used for quitting time was some small dinosaur.

Construction workers. Now it comes back to me—the reason my alarm bells rang like the small dinosaur at quitting time. Back when I was a detective, construction workers and long haul truckers were always red flags. If there was a dead girl, and some person of interest happened to be a construction worker or long haul trucker, they were put under the microscope. Red flag every time.

"Pancakes and bacon are served." She places the feast under my nose. I just stare. I'm afraid to break the spell I'm under because there's a chance that this feast is only in my imagination.

"You have syrup there next to the napkins." She places a hand on my shoulder and breaks me out of my spell. "Think of any other letters? From the license plate of that truck?"

"N." I empty half the syrup dispenser on my plate.

"Enjoy."

The first bite is indescribable. I fear the glorious pancakes are going to sever my train of thought so I force myself to lay the fork down and reengage with my inner detective.

Both jobs, construction workers and long

haul truckers, were almost entirely transient. Nomadic. Allowing for a free flow of movement that made it hard to discern a pattern. But a killer who stalks the same city or even the same geographic region, is a killer who develops a pattern. A pattern leads to a trail. Not so with transients. They come and go, off to a new city, and new killing grounds.

So, the guy I'm hunting has been careful to avoid leaving a pattern. Except one: a missing tooth. A trophy taken from both Daphne and...

Okay, wow. I realize I've finished my pancakes and bacon. And juice. I feel like I'm coming out of a coma. I blink several times and guzzle the last of my coffee.

The waitress clears my dishes and drops the bill at my elbow. "Did you think of any more letters, Sugar?"

"I did. I thought of the last letter."

"Oh, yeah? And what is it?"

"It's another A."

She winks. "L-A-N-A. Wait, that spells Lana."

The name of my daughter. I can see her face now.

Clear as day.

Lana.

Chapter Eighteen

Her gravestone reads:

Lana Matheson
1979-1999
An Angel Returned To Heaven

I sit facing it as rain falls on me. My new clothes are rumpled and drenched, hair matted across my skull.

The gravestone is made of travertine. The salesman told us it was from the same Italian quarry used for the Coliseum and Trevi Fountain. Even then I didn't understand the need for a gravestone made of Italian travertine. Just one more bad decision I let my ex-wife make. One more bad decision in a litany of bad decisions while I slipped away into oblivion.

So many memories...

I run my fingers across the engraving. The three t's are all halfway eroded, the crossbars fading. How is that possible? How could all of the other letters and numbers still hold their original form except for the t's?

I get the sudden impulse to find that salesman and drag him through the rain to Lana's grave and make him redo the t's. Maybe drag along my ex-wife as well.

"Do you see what Italian travertine got you? Do you see?!"

I picture Lana as the little girl I remember her to be. If I see her as anything older than fourteen, the gruesome details of her death come flooding back. So I prefer the little girl of seven, with blonde curls that nobody in either bloodline could explain. Her light brown eyes wise beyond their years, precocious and curious, trying to understand some of the mysteries that had puzzled great thinkers throughout the ages.

"Where did apple seeds come from, Daddy?"

"From apples."

"But the apples came from the seeds. What came first, Daddy?"

"You got me there, kiddo. Same as asking which came first, the chicken or the egg?"

"That's easy. The chicken."

"Why do you say chicken?"

"Because you can't have an egg unless the chicken lays it."

"But you can't have a chicken unless it hatches from an egg."

She shakes her head. "God created the chicken."

"Then did God create the apple first or the seed?"

She bites her lip, then pushes it out slowly, thinking, thinking...

Now I'm picturing her getting ready for her freshman year of high school. Thirteen. Her blonde curlycues have been shorn in favor of something called a pixie cut. Her short blonde hair frames her face and lets her cheekbones and little upturned nose really stand out. And her light brown eyes—still precocious, still curious—are now brimming with excitement and nerves.

She wanted to start high school with a new backpack, so we went to the K-mart and looked through the back-to-school aisles. Several other kids her age were browsing as well. A bright orange one caught her eye. My ex-wife tried talking Lana into some iron-on patches to give it flair. Favorite bands, TV shows, anything. But Lana didn't want to clutter up her bright orange canvas with momentary fads or crushes. I joked about finding an iron-on patch that said 'college or bust.'

Now I'm picturing her packing up for college. The University of Washington at Tacoma. She's just turned eighteen and has earned straight A's through high school, padding her GPA so she could gain admittance anywhere in the state. She chose Tacoma for its school of Environmental Science.

Her hair is now long and braided, having grown it out over the previous four years. I believe it was superstition that motivated her to let the hair keep going, a silly superstition that linked her academic achievement to the length of her hair. So every report card only reinforced the superstition and eight semesters and eight perfect report cards later, she wasn't about to let scissors or trimmers get anywhere near her beautiful blonde tresses.

"How're you going to be able to see what you're studying through that forest of hair?"

"That's what ties and scrunchies are for, Dad."

"Well, if the theater department puts on a production of Rapunzel, you've got yourself a nice Plan B."

"I'm not interested in Plan B. I have Plan A. That's the only plan," she said, keeping her eyes firmly on mine. As if she was dared me to challenge her—

Oh, no! No, no, no!

I've made the mistake of picturing her too old. Too close to the face that I found lying in the reservoir near our backyard. The face of my perfect student, on her way to becoming a perfect scientist who was going to finally determine whether the appleseed or the apple came first. All that perfection—strangled right out of her— lying down in the muck and weeds. Her face gray and bloated, mouth hanging open for a breath that never came. And the top front tooth ripped from her palate.

I punch the gravestone until my hand goes numb.

Chapter Nineteen

Now I'm working on a plan of my own. It's a hazy work-in-progress because my neuron pathways are sluggish with rust. Not to mention I now have a throbbing hand which is adding a level of distraction even as I try ignoring it.

I'm going to see Detective Hunan, the homicide detective assigned to Lana's case. The name swam up from the abyss as I sat weeping on my knees. Hunan, Hunan. She worked out of the same precinct as I did. I know where she lived and I'm heading there now. Twenty years later. Would she still be there? Would she, would she?

But it's dark and I've been rained on for hours. If I show up now, unannounced at night and soaking wet, it could sink my chances of reengaging with her. I might only have one chance at this.

My head is too full of cobwebs to know whether I'd ever crossed paths with Detective Hunan during my decades under the rock. Maybe she'd spotted me twice a week or maybe never at all. Either way, I'd be better served by giving myself an extra day to clean up and then call on her at an acceptable hour.

Maybe, maybe.

So now my plan is slightly altered. I turn away from the direction of her neighborhood and toward the Eighth Avenue Shelter instead. The sidewalks are slick and my bruised hand isn't gripping the crutch the way it should. I fear I might've fractured a metacarpal or two.

I arrive at the shelter even as the rain picks up. It is in the basement of a Presbyterian church. The doors close when all twenty-two beds are full so I'm happily surprised to find them still open and Miss Betty, the shelter supervisor, seated just inside the doorway.

"Gracious, you look like you swam through Noah's flood," she says, setting aside the Good Book she'd been reading. Miss Betty is an elderly little woman with big eyes and a big heart. She's one of the good ones, one who actually practices what she preaches.

"It's a hard rain, but not a Biblical one."

"True. God said one flood, and one flood only. The rainbow is our promise. Would you like help down to the basement?"

"I think I can manage." I attempt the first stair with my crutches but my bad hand slips off the handle and I grab the railing with my other hand to prevent a tumble down the stairs. Both crutches clatter down the tiled steps to the landing below.

Miss Betty is instantly at my elbow, taking some of the weight off my bad ankle. We hobble down the steps like a pair of drunks. She smells like lavender. Her hands are soft but her grip is firm.

We reach the landing and she picks up my crutches and hands them to me.

"Thank you, Miss Betty."

"You're very welcome. I pray a good night's sleep will mend your hand. But to help things along I'm going to hunt down an icepack. It'll just take a jiffy." She moves off down a hallway, toward the basement kitchen.

The cots are only half occupied. It's very unusual to see so many open cots on a rainy night. I recognize some of the faces hunkered down on the roll-away wafer-thin mattresses.

I choose one deepest in the basement, putting myself in a dark corner. I prefer corners to open space. Gives me an added sense of security, having my back against two walls. Maybe I was a homeless cowboy in another life.

I pass a black guy named Slim and his white sidekick, Benny. One of Slim's eyes is glass, made of bright green with a yellow iris. The same colors as his timeworn Supersonics parka. I think he prefers to live in the past, when Seattle still had a basketball team. Benny is a short-fry who always wears two bandanas, one red and one blue. Today he wears the red on his head like a second scalp and the blue fixed around his neck like a rustler about to hit a dusty trail.

"You make a loud entrance, buddy." Slim has a dry chortle, like his lungs are made of crepe paper.

"Sorry about that."

"I'm gonna lodge a complaint with the manager." Slim elbows his sidekick which triggers a forced laugh from Benny.

I plop onto my cot and the mattress exhales a cloud of dust and dander. "I'm under doctor's orders to be as loud as possible," I say just before a sneeze wells up and explodes into a cloud of my own spittle.

"Why does he want you to be loud?" Benny asks.

Slim and I exchange an amused look.

"He's kidding, goofball." Slim studies me. Even though I know his glass eye is cosmetic and not functional, it's unnerving when it moves up and down and all around. "There's something different about you. Like, you're giving off a different vibe or something. You're living in the here and now."

"Where was he living before?" Benny asks.

Miss Betty returns with a plastic baggie of ice. She sets it gently on my hand. I clasp her hand and give it a kiss.

She smiles and retreats to the staircase, where she pauses and turns to face all of us. "Welcome to Eighth Avenue Shelter. May I please start your night of peace and slumber with a prayer?" There are no dissenters. She bows her head. "Now I lay me down to sleep, I pray the Lord my soul to keep, If I should die before I wake, I pray the Lord my soul to take."

"Amen," we all say.

Chapter Twenty

I'm having a hard time nodding off.

My mind is preoccupied with thoughts of Lana. That's the price you pay when you choose to look back at old haunts. Also, something Slim said to me resonated. "You're living in the here and now."

Maybe I am, maybe I'm not. I don't know. The here and now kind of sucks. Living in a shelter kind of sucks. Knowing there is a killer out there sucks even more. Knowing your daughter's murderer is still out there, still killing, sucks worst of all.

I turn violently in bed, creaking the thing loudly.

The here and now. Yeah, that feels right. Not in a hole, not under a rock. Here. Now. In this place, at this time, in this body, in this mind. Peace, peace. Relax. Good, good. Breathe. Better, better.

One thing I do know is that I'll never find peace in the here and now. Then again, I didn't really find it under the rock or in the hole, or wherever the hell else my mind went to. I may never find peace again, but I could live with knowing I took this piece of shit off the streets.

The words "off the streets" reverberate in my mind, a small echo, and I hear them and see them, over and over and over...

When I do finally fall asleep, the dreams are a fusion of real and imaginary people, real places and not so real places. The dream people come with a sense of bittersweet nostalgia, as if my mind is stoking the embers of a fractured and false narrative. I liken it to seeing a movie a hundred times and then having the movie erased from your memory, but latent images and sounds still bleed into your waking thoughts.

One of the dream places is a cottage of some kind, near a lake or river. Although I never see the source of the water, I can sense it's nearby. Sometimes the cottage is made of flagstone, other times logs. The roof is usually shake shingles.

Inside the cottage, things seem less rustic. A player piano tinkles some slow and soft lullaby. Framed photographs on the wall, mostly sepia-tinted portraits of hazy folks I never take the time to inspect closely. A pot on the stove is sometimes filled with a stew, sometimes there's no kitchen at all. A bunkbed is in one corner, though sometimes it's a swinging hammock. This time it's the bunkbed, and it's occupied.

A little boy with a thick cowlick of black hair, wearing overalls, is dead asleep in the top bunk. I assume he's dead asleep, but I never see him move. Maybe he's just, well, dead.

Lying beneath on the bottom bunk is Miss Betty. She's looking right at me...

"Time to wake up, gentleman. It's almost noon. Up, up, up!" She eases out of the bottom bunk, tries rousting the boy in the top bunk. "Wake up! There you go. Good, good."

I wake up, too. And find Miss Betty standing over me. "You're the last one here, pal. I'm sorry for waking you, but you can't sleep here all day. Sorry. Rules are rules."

"I... I didn't realize how late it was."

"That's perfectly alright. How's the hand?"

I move my fingers. "A little stiff. I think I'll be able to play the piano."

"Oh, you play?"

I shrug. "I don't think so."

"Well, we have some leftover breakfast. How does scrambled eggs and toast sound?"

"Like heaven."

"I'll be back in a jiffy." She hurries to the kitchen down the hall.

The cots are all empty. Wow, okay. Dappling sunlight pours through the weed-choked window wells. I lie back down and replay the dream. Miss Betty is certainly new to my cast of dream people and places. She obviously leaked into my subconscious when the real Miss Betty intervened. But the boy...

That was the kicker. And like Miss Betty, he's never made an appearance until now. And he too is based on a real person. Definitely a real person.

He is me. I'm sure of it.

Chapter Twenty-one

On my way to Detective Hunan's house I realize I'm avoiding Briar Way, the street where the reservoir is located. The reservoir where Lana was found. It's the neighborhood where we used to live. Leafy and affluent. Old houses and stately trees. Lawns kept immaculate by hired landscapers.

I'm tired of avoidance, tired of being repelled by my own fear. I've not seen the reservoir in twenty years. All the time under that damn rock, I never once visited it. Never took a step onto Briar Way.

Facing down your demons is the most personal battle you can wage. Now I'm ready.

Time to link the here and now with the there and then.

My feet get heavier the closer I get. My body feels a physical resistance, as if I'm walking against a 40 mph wind. My blood quickens. Forehead and hands sweating, lips bone dry. I wet them with my tongue.

The old chain-link fence is still standing between the sidewalk and the reservoir. The fence goes all the way around. There's an access gate that's kept padlocked. The killer had thrown Lana over the fence, then jumped the fence after her. We found the evidence.

I catch myself at the corner of the fence line. I'm wobbly. I drop the crutches, grip the chain links, and make my way to the center of the barrier. There I cling to it, staring down to the marshy bank where her body had been left to rot. From here, I can see the spot where she'd been found, partially buried in the swampy earth. She'd been partially covered in twigs and branches and mud. The sinking had more to do with the marshy land itself.

Two bodies, both partially buried. Both half-assed efforts.

My mind's eye can also see the imprints of the boots worn by her killer. We'd recovered about fifteen usable prints from where he'd jumped down off the fence and then dragged her down to the water's edge. I was still hopeful and competent at that stage. Trying to be respectful of Hunan's space, but constantly pushing for more progress. I had a timer in my head that counted down, screaming at me to find that monster before he slipped into the shadows and was gone forever.

I'd started to drink then... literally the next day. My ex-wife wasn't judging me yet because she was using other substances to cope. But when I started drinking on the job a week or so later, that was when the case and I began floundering. Every day that went by without an arrest—or even a person of interest—I would get to drinking earlier and heavier.

The boots he'd worn had been a size 13 Timberlands. Waterproof. Otherwise unremark-able. Tracing their purchase would've been like hunting down a Big Mac wrapper to its source McDonald's.

The prints did reveal other information. They told us he was left-handed/footed. His stride was the size of someone six-foot-two or six-foot-three. About 245 pounds.

The way he'd positioned Lana was another set of signifiers.

He'd killed her prior to the reservoir. This was just the dump site. The drag marks from her body all pointed to a lifeless Lana.

He left her face-up, which meant he wasn't trying to hide his crime, nor did he feel remorse or shame. She'd been staged in a slumbering position, to show she was at peace. Yeah, right. And then, for reasons that could only point to the macabre, he'd ripped her front incisor from her mouth. This was a souvenir. A trophy. We all knew it. Lana knew it most of all.

And trophy killers are never one-offs. After all, trophies are intended to be part of a collection. This guy had killed before and was going to kill again.

Two decades he's been free to kill while I floundered and suffered and hid.

No more, dammit. No more.

I took in some air. Held it.

"No fucking more."

Chapter Twenty-two

Detective Grace Hunan lives in a grand old Tudor-style home.

If, of course, she still lived here.

It has a sweeping roofline and dark brown trim with little decorative windows that remind me of frosted panes in ski chalets. The driveway is newly sealed and the window boxes and gardens are full of bright lively flowers. It's the house of someone who takes extraordinary care over matters. The same trait that made her a good homicide detective.

If, of course, she still lived here.

I approach the front door, tempted to grab some flowers from the garden to present as an ice-breaker. But then rethink it. She'd instantly recognize them from her own garden. She'd probably accept them gracefully as she scanned for the fresh gaps I'd just pulled them from. She was too classy to show naked reproach, but I'd receive only her basic social niceties.

If, of course, she still lived here.

I've been standing on the front porch for over a minute, my mind a train wreck of images and remembrances. Grace had been quite lovely back in the day. We had been neighbors and I'd often seen her jogging through the neighborhood. She'd pause and we would talk, usually about work, though we weren't partners. A fluke that she got my daughter's case. Could have been anyone. Well, anyone but me.

The memories, crystal clear, no longer swimming up from the depths, but there, right there, front and center. I breathe, sway, balance myself.

I'm feeling the same polar opposites I'd experienced back at the reservoir: My forehead and hands are sweating, my mouth is bone dry. I ring the doorbell. It has a small camera embedded in the housing. My heart beats too fast, too hard, in my ears, in my head, in my teeth. If I walk away now on the crutches I'd only reach the sidewalk before she answered the door and caught me slinking away like some weirdo.

After an agonizing forty-five seconds, the door opens. And there she is, Grace Hunan. Her hair has gone snow white, and her face has doubled the age lines since my last memory of her. She's still gorgeous. Her body still fit, I think. I can see she's drawing a blank for me. See the wariness. But also the strength. She's not one to mess with. There would be a gun nearby, of course.

"Can I help you?" she asks.

Her hard expression softens for some reason. Recognition? Maybe, maybe.

"Detective Hunan, I'm sorry for the umm…" Tripped up by my cotton mouth. Certain sounds are not easy to form without saliva to help them along. I wait for my glands to produce some lubricant for my tongue. She waits and watches, her gaze amused. Not frightened. Just patient and curious, curious.

"My name is James Matheson. I was a detective once at…"

Her face cracks with a smile. "James? How are you? How long has it been?"

I'm shaking her hand. I have an impulse to give her a peck on the cheek but it seems overly familiar and I haven't kissed anyone in, well, a very long, long time. I'm not even sure I remember how.

"Um, I've been away for a while. Several years." I keep it vague and watch to see if she reveals any sign that she's aware of my long residence under the rock. But she keeps her face open and inviting. Another prized trait for a homicide detective: keep the witness feeling that he's among friends.

"What brings you to my neck of the woods?"

"That is a question I should have thought of before I rang your bell." I look at my feet and sway side to side on the crutches. I'm at a loss for words. My mind had been so focused on ringing her doorbell that I hadn't planned my next move. Relax, relax.

"You're here about your daughter."

I nod and try to speak but tears burst from my eyes.

"Oh, James."

And now she's hugging me and I weep into the curve of her neck, my arms hanging down at my sides. She pulls me in tighter and tighter, and I do not know how long we stand like that, or care.

Chapter Twenty-three

I am all cried out. For now.

Meanwhile, she leads me inside into her living room. Her house is as manicured and fashionable as expected. No, as I remember. Well, kinda. I'd been inside her home maybe three times before. A Christmas party once. Two times to discuss my daughter's case. Those hadn't been nice meetings. Room is different now, darker. Lots of grainy wood with little color. Depressing avant-garde cubism paintings on the wall. One looks like a knight who'd been sliced and diced and put together at odd angles. Not a single flower anywhere. No color anywhere. Hard to stay upbeat doing what we did, investigating the worst of mankind. She offers me a seat on her mocha-colored couch. I drop down, sink into the leather.

I take a moment to look around the room. Not many photos from which to draw information about her current relationship status, although the house has a sensation of emptiness, as if we're its only two occupants.

She takes a seat on a matching leather recliner. She waits until I'm done with my snooping.

"You okay?"

"Yes, no, not really."

She nods, understanding. Homicide detectives deal with the full gambit of emotions each and every day, though I suspect she is retired now.

"Other than that, how have you been? What have you been doing with yourself?"

What to share, what to not share What did she know? Was it common knowledge that I'd disappeared from common society? My degeneration had been slow. A process of maybe a year. Most would have assumed I moved or lived with family members or lived in an insane asylum. My breakdown had been no secret. My collapse had been evident for all to see.

"I'm no longer in the neighborhood. You probably knew that." I wipe my hands on my thighs. The pants seem too baggy and I wonder if she's noticed my bony knees. Had she already deduced my long bout of homelessness and instability? I look her in the eyes again and decide to forget about trying to maintain any false fronts. I am what I am, I became what I became. I did my best to just survive, to cope, to deal, to live. Forget maintaining any semblance of ego or foolish pride. I'd rather be open and honest with her. Grace Hunan, over the many years I'd had dealings with her, had always struck me as someone whose character started and ended with genuine humanity.

"I've been on the streets for a long time, actually, Grace. I wasn't able to withstand the tailspin after... Lana." My eyes well up again. I don't fight it. That would be a false front.

Her own eyes brim over as well. She has become a softy with age. "I've heard rumors, James. I... didn't want to believe them."

I shake my head. "Not as bad as you think. Okay maybe exactly as bad as you think. Maybe even a little worse. But it got me here, alive and ready."

"Ready for what?"

"To catch the bastard."

"James... that was over twenty years ago. He's long gone. Probably dead."

I shake my head and rock back and forth on the sofa. He's back, he's back.

Am I speaking or thinking? I don't know; I don't know.

I rock and rock and rock, hearing myself mumble under my breath. The hole is near, so is the rock. Pull it together, James, together, together.

She reaches out and pats my hand. "You've had a hard time, James."

I nod and rock.

"I'm sorry I couldn't find the killer. My guess was he was a transient. We hunted everywhere for the bastard. Everywhere we could think of. I worked this case harder than any other case. I still think about it."

Deep breaths, good, good.

I nod and keep nodding. "You... you did your best. All of you did."

She sits back and pulls her feet onto the recliner, tucking them under herself, studying me. It's a sign of comfortable familiarity. Like letting your hair down. I don't know if she's consciously trying to put me at ease, but she is. "There were no leads, James. None at all. I'm so sorry."

I run my hands through my graying hair, nodding, nodding. "No... no reason to be sorry. I know you did your best."

She wipes her cheeks, looking more petite than I remember. "Can I get you something,

James? A tea or coffee?"

"No... thank you." I don't know whether I should push my agenda any further. I think she's trying to let me down gently, informing me she's not prepared to dig up old cases.

"The case on Lana didn't, ah, progress in the intervening years since you left the department. There were some decent leads that I followed, but like so much of that case, everything got swallowed up in the static." Her hands are very emotive, moving back and forth with her fingers opening and interlocking. She waits until our eyes are connecting before she continues. "What would you need from me, James?"

I try to smile, not knowing if I do or not. "I didn't have a list prepared..."

"This is going better than you expected, huh?" She chuckles lightly. "Look, I do have some stuff I keep in a storage unit. Cold case stuff that were my greatest misses. Some boxes I didn't feel comfortable leaving behind in the evidence lock-up."

This is unexpected, and music to my ears. I sit forward.

"Can we set up a follow-up visit?" she asks. "Give me a couple days to sift through my storage unit and collect the relevant files?"

"Yes, please. Thank you."

"I'm happy to help you, James. Lana

deserves a better ending than the one she got. And so do you."

I wipe my eyes and reach for my crutches.

"If you don't mind my asking... was there something that triggered this renewed interest? I mean, I haven't heard or seen you in twenty years, James."

It's a great question, direct and intuitive. I get to my feet, stumbling slightly. "Another girl."

"Lots of dead girls out there, James."

"She's missing a front tooth."

She lowers her gaze and sweeps it across the floor. I can see her mind at work, synthesizing new information with the old. *Once a detective, always a detective.*

"Where was the body found?"

"Grant's Park. A partial burial, staged."

Her eyes widen ever so slightly. "Let me make some inquiries. I've still got close contacts in the department."

I nod, too eager and excited to know what to say. Her hand touches my lower back, guiding me to the front door.

"James, it is good seeing you. I only wish it could have been under different circumstances."

There is a glint in her eye. Interest? Compassion? Curiosity? I decide to do something I haven't done in nearly forty years... twenty on the streets, and twenty in marriage. I decide to test the waters. "I'm sorry I wasn't able to see your husband again. Charlie was it?"

I step out the front door and turn back. Her mood has darkened. I've pushed too far forward and stepped on a landmine. Or not. What do I know?

"Charlie, yes. That was his name." It's her turn to tear up. "He passed almost six years ago. Colon cancer. It's why I retired early, so I could care for him."

"I'm so sorry, Grace." I feel the deepest urge to draw her into my arms. It's almost a physical ache, my desire to hold her. "I didn't know."

"Like you said, you were out of the loop." She leans against the door frame. Again, a display of comfortable familiarity. "So Thursday night? Say 6 o'clock? I'll have dinner ready, too, if that's okay. I make a mean lasagna."

I have to speak around the lump in my throat. "Thursday at six."

I turn and work my way down the porch steps, smiling, smiling.

Smiling.

Chapter Twenty-four

I walk out of my old neighborhood with a spring in my step.

Not literally. I'll never have a *real* spring in my step again—my bad ankle has seen to that. But I'm so happy that it feels like I'm walking on sunshine.

Reacquainting with Grace Hunan had gone better than my wildest expectations. She was empathetic and eager to help. We had some promising chemistry, and our shared history was a nice safety net to any of the awkward moments.

I have two days to get myself even more presentable. I think I should start with my friend in the RV, Annie. I don't know if that's her real name, but she seems like an Annie to me. Friends usually know each other's names, so I'll think of her as Annie until she tells me different. Or I could be a good detective and get it on the sly. Trick her into revealing it without tipping my hat...

It feels good to be using my brain for something more than keeping my neck dry. I like the world outside of the rock.

I also have the Eighth Avenue Shelter and Miss Betty to fall back on. The church has a small bathroom in the basement that includes a shower. I'm going to need to shower daily from now on. A fresh set of clothes and a shower every day. It seems like such a burden. A foreign act to the way I'd been living. It must require at least half an hour to shave your face and clean your body and put on a set of clean clothes. But if that's how regular society operates, and if I'm interested in being included again, I need to conform.

The red-light district is on my way to all points south, be it the park or Annie's or the shelter. So I decide to check back in with the ladies of the night. I told them I'd be looking into Daphne's murder, and I want them to see that my word is my bond. Prove to them that I wasn't just shooting off my mouth about finding justice for Daphne.

I reach the street corner but it's empty. Somewhat unusual for late afternoon. I take a lap around the intersection and peer into each alley. No business is being conducted in the shadows, and no negotiations are happening near idling cars.

My scalp feels the familiar prickles. Something's not right. But where do I go from here? The women don't have a union hall or professional guild. Nobody outside their parasitic pimp would be able to explain why their "lobby" is closed.

The only real course of action is to sit tight and wait for somebody to come forward. The nearest bus stop bench is one block over, in the shadow of the construction site. Which means I can kill two birds with one stone: 1) watch and wait for the red-light district to open for business, and 2) watch and wait to see if anybody at the construction site is overly interested in what's happening a block to the east.

But when I reach the construction site, I notice some police flashers off in the distance, strobing through the trees that border the neighborhood and partition off the park. I hurry down the block toward the flashers. When I arrive at the tree line and wrought iron fence, I spot a crowd massing near the big fountain in the park. Squad cars—marked and unmarked—

and an ambulance are assembled on the fountain's cobblestone apron.

I push my way through the throngs of bystanders, all the way to the police tape that cordons off a section of park that's being photographed and culled by detectives from my old precinct. I don't recognize any of them, but I do spot the two black prostitutes I'd been searching for. They're standing just outside the tapeline. The tall one with the big blonde mane is dabbing at the tears in her eyes. The shorter one with the pot belly is scowling, either in anger or impatience. Then I see what they're reacting to:

A coroner's white blanket is covering a body lying at the edge of a row of poplar trees. The curvaceous contours of the corpse can't be concealed by the fleece blanket…

It's the stunning woman in the white catsuit.

Chapter Twenty-five

I work my way over to the pair of women.

The short one sees me first. Her scowl remains fixed: not even a single twitch to her expression. The taller one sees me and holds her hands out for mine, wiggling her long scarlet fingernails in anticipation of my grasp.

"Superman! Flying in for the reckoning!"

I clutch her hands and she melts into my shoulder, body trembling. She's crying on my shoulder. I hold her patiently, awkwardly. The short one pops her chewing gum and rolls her eyes.

"Tie it off, Blondie, or you're going to waste all your fluids on some gimp's shoulder."

Blondie—if that's indeed her name—breaks off contact and wipes her eyes, careful to not blind herself with her red claws.

"When did they find the body?" I ask.

"About lunchtime," the short ones replies.

"And how was she killed?"

"Strangled." She shrugs, pops another bubble.

Blondie looks back to the covered corpse. "She was too beautiful for the street. She belonged on a stage or a..."

"Pole," offers the short one.

Blondie hisses at her. "Be respectful."

"What was her name?" I ask.

"Coco," they say together.

"That her real name or her street name?"

Blondie shrugs. "We never exchanged anything too personal. Just surfacy stuff."

"How long had she been working the area?"

"Ever since Daphne got gone," the short one says.

"He's got a type," Blondie says.

I give her an approving nod. Good detective work. "Have you thought anymore about people you'd seen Daphne with right up to the time she was killed? Or Coco? Anybody who stands out for any reason?"

"You sound like a cop. Your questions and your attitude." The short one tilts her head like she's trying to see me from a different angle. "Are you a cop?"

"Ex-detective."

The short one sneers and the tall one claps excitedly. They are true opposites in every way.

"I worked out of this precinct. This neighborhood, as a matter of fact."

"When?"

"A long time ago."

"What happened?" Blondie asks, riveted.

"I'd like to focus on Coco and Daphne, if we could. Do either of you recall anything that stands out recently? Anything that might've seemed mundane or normal at the time, but now —in light of her murder—seems suspicious or out of the ordinary?"

They both shake their heads.

I believe them. They've got nothing to help things along. But I can feel my detective swagger coming back. The conversation with Grace gave my confidence a boost. Sometimes when you're about to catch a wave, you need to let yourself float in the moment and be ready for wherever the ride is going to take you. Far, far, far different than being under the rock.

Better, so much better.

"Wait," says shorty. "She was talking to the horns dogs."

"Horn dogs?" I ask.

"The construction workers," adds Blondie, nodding toward the street corner where I'd recently spent time observing. "But lots of us talk to them."

Shorty shakes her head. "She took a fancy to one."

"Do you remember which one?" I ask.

"Hard hat and white."

"Tall, short? Old, young?"

"Don't remember."

"Did Daphne talk to the horn dogs, too?"

"Don't remember, but probably. Like Blondie says, we talk to all sorts of guys. Even gimps."

They're each carrying a tiny purse and a thought occurs to me. "You always carry those little handbags?"

"Of course," Blondie says with a wink. "We keep the tools of our trade in here."

Nodding, I say, "Good, add something else to your tool bags. They sell tiny cans of pepper spray at the convenience store down the road on a key chain."

Shorty gives me a guarded look and Blondie nods solemnly.

I thank the ladies and tell them I might stop by again. Blondie says she would like that. Shorty is already moving away from the crime scene, having lost interest. Life on the streets.

Turning my attention to the crime scene, I see the photographer and forensics guys are wrapping up. The light is failing and they're about to lose out to the stampede of foot traffic that's pushing against the tapeline. The body has been transferred onto a gurney as the techs wheel it toward the ambulance.

I move along the tapeline, staying parallel with the crime scene guys and the rolling body. I'm aware that I won't be able to intercept them, but I'm pushing to get as near as possible to where our paths will almost converge.

I move within arm's reach. I have an urge to whip back the blanket and see for myself if Coco's missing a tooth. But I realize the risk is not worth the reward. So I do the next stupidest thing and raise my voice: "Excuse me, could you tell me whether or not the victim is missing one of her front teeth?"

The crime scene momentarily freezes. I see the techs make eye contact with each other, and then with the detectives, who're all swooping in my direction.

Even with two good feet I wouldn't try breaking away. But it would've been nice to have the option.

A burly guy in a houndstooth jacket steps over the tape and into my personal bubble. He's got a fresh crewcut and a steno pad.

"Hello, sir, how're you this evening?"

To my right, Blondie and Shorty melt into the crowd. They are as good as gone. I don't blame them. After all, I just made the dumbest, most rookie mistake: I provided information that the police would never publicly release. So I just got flagged as a potential suspect.

Another detective and a uniform are now behind me. I've just talked myself into a trip to the station house. I could try and argue my innocence, clarify how I got my information and my ties to the case. But that would be a lot of laundry to air out in the open.

"Am I going for a ride so you can ask me some questions?"

"Gee, how did you know?" He nods to the uniform.

"Sir, you're not being placed under arrest and I am not mirandizing you. We are just transporting you to the station for questioning. Do you understand?"

"Am I being handcuffed?"

I can see a quick meeting of eyes between the lead detective and the uniform.

"No, sir. That's not necessary, as long as you continue making it not necessary."

"I understand. I don't want to be cuffed."

The detective nods, and I'm led to a squad car and loaded into the back. The uniform is being extra patient, waiting for me and my leg to get situated before handing me my crutches through the open door.

I scan the crowd as we push through it, and spot something that makes me sit up. I turn in my seat, desperate for another look, but it's too late. The crowd swallows him up. But I know what I saw. I know it, I know it.

A man standing just behind the crowd. A man with a construction helmet under one arm. Watching the procession of police vehicles.

And grinning.

Chapter Twenty-six

They said I wasn't being arrested, but they could've fooled me.

Other than not reading me my rights and not fingerprinting me, the rest of the routine was pretty much as I remembered it. Only this time, I was catching and not pitching.

Eventually, I end up in an interrogation room, where a Lieutenant Barnes subjects me to much hostile questioning. When he's done throwing his weight around, he learns that I'm ex-homicide; in fact, I used to work out of this very station. The junior detective blinks, squints, consults his notes, and verifies my name. He asks if I remember my shield number. I do, and give it to him.

He jots it down and tells me to sit tight, leaving me alone in the very room I'd used to question countless witnesses. Cracked cement floor, drain in the back, vent in the corner of the ceiling, though I feel no air moving. One-way mirror to my right. Older than I remember, more intimidating. Then again, I'd been on the other side of the fence, so to speak.

I sit quietly and bow my head and think about God, and thank Him for my newfound clarity, for allowing my badge number to swim up from the depths, for giving me a chance to bring this whole sad affair to a conclusion. God knew the killer's identity. God loved the killer, too. Was Lana with God now?

I hoped so; I hope so.

Please, please.

I stare at the cinderblock wall for over thirty minutes. Maybe longer, maybe shorter. They don't put clocks in interrogation rooms. I'm not handcuffed to the table. My stomach rumbles, and I pat it. Patting it doesn't help, maybe even makes it worse. I have fourteen dollars. Lots and lots and lots of food I can buy with fourteen dollars.

The door opens and the female detective who had spoken to me at Grant's Park last week walks in. She smiles at me. She sits across from me and sets what I assume is my personnel file on the table between us.

"We meet again, Mr. Matheson. Or should I say Detective? Do you remember me?"

"Yes."

"Do you remember my name?"

"No, sorry."

"I didn't expect you would. When we last we spoke you were unable to even remember your own name. Barnes tells me you just rattled off your old badge number without a second thought."

"Last week had been the beginning of my, ah, awakening."

"What does that mean?"

"Since finding Daphne, I've gone through some changes."

"What kind of changes?"

"Head clearing, memory returning."

She studies me, squinting. She is pretty, hard around her lips, but with kind eyes. A good combination to crack any case, surely. "You clean up well, Mr. Matheson."

"Please, call me James."

She squints some more. I suspect she doesn't understand what she's seeing. She will soon enough, if she's good at her job. She opens the file before her. I see hand written notes at the top of the file. Her notes? Probably.

"You appear to have dropped off the map

twenty years ago, James. That's about the last time you made a mortgage payment, utility payment and a car payment. Your car was repossessed shortly after, and the bank foreclosed on your home a year later. You were last seen in the Fairbank institution in Mont Lake, where you walked out one day and never returned."

"Seems about right."

She looks up. "Have you been living on the streets ever since, James?"

"Streets, alleys, shelters, parks, bus stations, sidewalks. A few backyards. Abandoned houses. Barns a little further outside the city, back before I broke my ankle."

She folds her hands over the open file, a wedding band on her ring finger. She's dressed in slacks and a loose blouse. Badge on her hip. Gun probably at her desk.

"You lost everything," she says simply.

"I lost my little girl. Yes, everything. Everything else is just noise."

"Reminders?"

"Maybe."

"You lost your wife too."

"She left me. I don't blame her. It was a rough time for both of us."

"Might have been rougher on you," she says.

I shrug. "Who's to say?"

"Your wife remarried, started another family."

I open my mouth to speak, close it, then try again. "I am happy for her."

"Last week you were delusional, rambling, crying, dirty, broken. What changed?"

"Finding Daphne."

"You were friends with her."

Half shrug. "She was kind to me, nothing more."

"Her murder had similarities with your daughter."

"Yes."

"The missing tooth."

"And the shallow burial, the staging of the body."

"Seeing her awakened something within you," she says.

"Yes."

"Something you tried to bury deep."

"Yes." My voice cracks.

"You are back now."

"Yes, and no. As back as can be, perhaps. There are..."

"Yes?"

"Still moments of confusion, delusion."

"I can understand that."

We are silent for a moment.

"Are you working both cases?" I ask. "Daphne and Coco?"

"For now, yes."

"Was Coco missing a tooth, too?"

She holds my gaze for a long time. "Yes. And I would only say this to a fellow detective."

"Thank you. But it's been a long time since I worked a case."

"You are working this one now, aren't you?"

"I am. As best as I can, with the resources I have."

"Did Ms. Hunan agree to help you?"

"She did, yes."

"Officially, I have to ask you to stand down."

"I understand." I wait, ask. "And unofficially?"

"Unofficially, I hope you find this piece of shit."

I take in some air, slowly, slowly. "Was Coco buried in a shallow grave, too?"

"Yes."

"Staged?"

"A strange pose this time, like she'd died modeling on the Price is Right. Clues are still coming in."

We are silent for a while. Only the faint

buzz of the halogens overhead give any indication that sound still exists in the world. I nearly tell her about my construction yard lead, but I don't for reasons I don't quite understand.

No, I do understand. I do, I do.

I want to find him myself.

I want to find him. I want to find him. I want to find him.

She talks to me some more, gently, asking about my life, about where I'm living, my health. She asks about my ankle too, and I see her mind working. She knows I am holding back on her, knows that I'm onto something, knows there's a reason why I happened to be near the second victim, knows that I am closing in on the killer. I hope so, I hope so.

Shortly, she walks me through the station and out the main entrance. She hands me a package she'd been carrying. Something wrapped in a paper bag. From the weight, I know it's my gun.

"Old thing," she says. "Single shot. Make it count."

I open my mouth to speak, perhaps even to protest.

I close it again. After all, there's nothing to protest. Or, really, anything to say.

She asks if I want a ride and I decline. The walk will give me time to think, I say. She nods and heads back inside. I watch her through the smoky glass door until I can't see her any more.

I pocket my gun, adjusts the crutches, and head for the shelter.

Chapter Twenty-seven

Never shit where you sleep. And never dump bodies where you work.

Maybe I should have revealed the Hard Helmet guy to the detective, but I don't need a competing stakeout. If too many cop cars—marked or otherwise—troll the red-light district, the guy could get spooked. Although a guy who suddenly bugs out when the building isn't even half finished would be a sure tell.

Maybe I'd need to get cozy with the fore-man. He or she would be a great resource to lean on. It was another thing to be added to my mental to-do list. I enjoyed the logistics of an investigation. I'd always liked putting together the strategy and aligning resources at the outset.

It was stimulating. Riveting. Because in the early stages, everything is promising. Every lead seems to inch you ever closer to a possible break.

But the difference now was that I didn't have to deal with bureaucracy. Nobody checking my work or second guessing my hunches. The pecking order of a police investigation could be suffocating. Although you had every possible resource at your disposal, including manpower, the trade off was guys like Lieutenant Barnes who wanted to swing his dick around and mark as much territory as possible. A case often takes a backseat to their egos.

A lot of police are egotists. And detectives are egotists with a license to dig through your shit until they find something that can be used against you. I tried to never let my ego dictate my actions. But the power can be intoxicating. Barnes was practically drunk with his own importance.

I was making a lot more noise around town than I'd intended. It's dangerous to suddenly emerge from nowhere and poke around in police business. But I had an ally with... she never told me her name. Detective No-name it is, then.

Chapter Twenty-eight

I awaken early the next morning.

It's still dark, and the prospect of a warm breakfast is enticing—I can smell the bacon and eggs already in the skillet—but I need to be at the construction site at daybreak. I need to see the parade of vehicles as they arrive.

I get dressed in yesterday's duds, already disappointing myself for breaking my vow of wearing a fresh set of clothes every day. But that vow takes a backseat to the investigation. Everything must take a backseat now. I'm fully engaged with the case, my mind pulsing with the too-long dormant electricity that comes with the opening phase of a new investigation.

Yes, that's how I see this... a new investigation.

A new investigation with old ties.

I think of the old ties, not fully, not completely, just enough to see the connections.

The hole, the hole. It's so close, so terrible, so deep.

Breathe, focus, good, good.

Dressed and focused, I hurry to the corner bus bench, feeling like I have wind at my back and a full sail pushing me along. Fifteen minutes, I depart carefully, hopping and limping and crutching. Once on solid ground, the bus driver waves to me, sadness in her eyes. My smile says there's no need for sadness. Today is a new day.

A half a block later I'm where I want to be, more than any place on this planet.

I sigh, relax, find a low wall to park my behind on.

The construction site is lifeless. My guess is it's just after 7a.m. Who needs a watch? The light in the sky is enough, even if this will likely be a cloudy day. The texture of the light, the brightness, the depth in the clouds is enough. No, I didn't often need to know the time. But I got to the point where telling it had become second nature. Maybe not so much when in the hole, but any other times, yes.

Yes, yes, yes.

The building under construction now has two added levels of I-beams since the first afternoon I noticed the leering behavior of the welders. The barrier wall that circumnavigates the site's entire footprint is a great hindrance to my surveillance. The workers' personal vehicles can give me vital information, but I only have access to them in two small windows: as they arrive and as they depart.

Thirty minutes later, they do just that... arrive.

Oh, yes, yes.

As they do so, I open the newspaper I'd snatched from the trash on the walk over here. Now, as I sit, I use the daily crossword puzzle to take down license plate numbers as the work ers arrive. Most vehicles are pick-up trucks. Not sure what the percentage of construction workers who drive pickup trucks is, but it's got to be in the eighty to ninety percentile range here today.

The vast majority of vehicles are in-state. Although my dictation isn't fast enough to write down the plate number of every vehicle that enters the site, I make it a point to jot down the out-of-state tags.

Out of forty-three vehicles, four are from neighboring states: two from Idaho, one from Oregon, and one from California.

An out-of-state tag represents a red flag. Somebody who would murder two streetwalkers within a week of one another and dump their bodies so close to each other, is someone who feels emboldened by a cloak of impermanence. They'd never conduct such brazen behavior if they intended to stick around. Patterns are only incriminating if you continue the pattern in proximity.

I could use the out-of-state tags to track DMV records in order to pinpoint permanent residences, then cross-reference those residences against other open investigations of murdered young women missing a front tooth, the odds of getting any real meaningful break would be astronomical—needle-in-the-haystack odds. There's just too much static in which to find a clear signal.

Of course, that would also mean I had access to DMV and inter-departmental databases, which I don't.

No, I don't... but Grace Hunan, retired private detective extraordinaire, might. Though not directly. Surely after just six years off the force, she had reliable contacts. And didn't I possible, possibly, have a friend in Detective No-name. Yeah, maybe. Except I don't know her name.

Easy to fix, easy to fix. Grace will know, or

can find out.

Yes, yes.

Breathe, good, good.

For now, on my own, I have to use the out-of-state tags as an indicator, not as a first step in a sequence of further steps, though that could come later with luck, and with some help.

I nod to myself, and keep nodding. Yes, yes.

These are the hunches one can follow if one is working solo. If I had somebody to answer to —or even a partner to collaborate with—such a hunch would have to be vigorously defended. But I don't have to defend anything now, do I? No, no.

I'm going to ride my hunch as if it's a bucking steer that needs to be wrangled for a brief period of wild activity.

Meanwhile, the sun begins to make its slow rise up the eastern sky. The sound of diesel engines and rivet guns and welding torches all mix into a symphony of rumbles and thrumming and hammering.

A good day.

Yes, yes.

Chapter Twenty-nine

I spend another hour waiting for late arrivals.

Nobody else shows up except for a couple architects. They drive pick-ups as well, but high-end, their truck beds are immaculate because they've never really been used.

By the time the welders are back up in the structure's higher reaches, making their showers of incandescent sparks, I decide to catch breakfast at Finley's. I'm still holding nine dollars out of the twenty. The place smells like heaven again, but the angel who waited on me last time isn't here. Instead, it's a younger Latina. Very pretty, but very straightforward.

"What can get I get you?"

"Eggs and bacon, coffee and OJ."

She and I keep things cordial but all business. From my table next to the window, I watch the construction site's activity across the street. Nothing of note happens. The workers are completely anonymous. I'm unable to categorize or profile anybody. And without differentiating the population into categories of probable to longshot, my observation time isn't being spent usefully.

If I was with the department, I could get on a neighboring high-rise and get some quality observation time.

My stomach full and my wallet's near empty, I'm about to exit when I get a sudden impulse.

"Excuse me," I say to the Latina. "Could you tell me how long the building across the street has been going up?"

The Latina waitress takes the pencil from behind her ear and rubs its eraser on her temple. "Months. Maybe five or six."

"Five or six months. Is there any way you can better pinpoint the start date? Maybe by using something from your personal life to help put the start date into context?"

She's taken aback. I think I've creeped her out. Occupational hazard. Even if I was active police with ID and a shield, she might still be feeling uneasy. I decide to not push.

"I know. Sometimes it's hard to remember. But five or six months, you say?"

She nods, shrugging.

"That's very helpful. Have a good day."

I step out into the late morning and walk between the construction site and the park. It takes me less than five minutes on crutches. Someone with two good legs can make it in a fraction of the time. The pieces are becoming fixed in my head: the guy works at the construction site.

One of the four with out-of-state tags.

I'm sure of it.

The angle I need to work now is finding out whether anybody else from the red-light district went missing in the past six months. Such an attack would represent a pilot killing: an experimental murder to determine whether any real heat was generated. If the police didn't make enough of an effort, and the killer didn't feel threatened, it would've represented a green light...

If so, it was open season.

Chapter Thirty

I have time to kill before my next window of opportunity. I use it to canvas the park, nosing around for anything that might open another lead in my investigation.

But the time spent there is a violent upheaval to my psyche. Every inch of that park comes with a long and tortured replay of blurry days spent shambling from one self-induced misery to another, year after year, until the net gain from my life within the wrought iron fence line is a mangled foot and a long, slow slide into insanity.

At the big multi-tiered fountain near the spot where the most recent body had been found, I picture myself taking a soak in the water's jets, sometimes naked but more often clothed. At the park bench behind the rows of poplar trees I can see myself lying all nestled up, breath steaming, as I try desperately and futilely to generate more body warmth. Near the fish pond I can recall scrounging shamelessly through the various waste baskets for sustenance, even contending with the ducks for the scraps of bread donated by park-goers.

I shake my hands at the thought of running ducks off food I would sit and eat near the garbage.

I'm alive, I'm alive. I made it, I made it.

It's okay, okay.

No, no.

Yes, yes.

Breathe, breathe.

Can't, can't, can't, can't.

I weep at the images, run my fingers through my neatly trimmed hair.

The hole, hole, hole... right there behind me.

Breathe, it's okay. Good, good.

Breath. Ah, yes, yes.

I stand there breathing and running my hands through my hair, crutches under my arms, light weight resting on my embattled foot. How long I stand there, I don't know. Judging by the slant of light, maybe an hour, maybe less.

I leave the park none too soon. Clearly, it's not a good place for me to revisit. Whether or not I've truly cleared out the decades-old fog that had ensnared me, retracing old steps in the park is like walking against a moving sidewalk: progress is stilted or possibly even reversed.

I shambled back to the bench across from the construction site, eager to put the park behind me. Once situated and relaxed and feeling back to my new self, I watch the activity before and above me. When I notice the welders taking time to observe the street corner one block over, I realize it's time to go and talk with my two gal pals, Blondie and Shorty.

I don't know their actual names. Making personal connections has never been my strong suit. But a good investigator is open to any road that might take them another step closer to that big break in the case.

The tall blonde one with the Adam's Apple is wearing a yellow backless mini-dress and bright purple pumps. The other one is again in her black leather short-shorts and bra, now accented with fish-net stockings and a black leather baseball cap with the word *Princess* in white rhinestones.

They're standing on the same spot where I'd originally approached them. It's only been a matter of days, but they seem like old friends at this point. And as I make my way toward them, I can see they share my feelings. Even the short angry one curls her mouth into a half-smile.

"Good afternoon, ladies."

"Superman!" Blondie claps while jumping up and down. I've never gotten such a gleeful welcome in my whole life.

"What do you say, Mr. Detective?" Shorty asks, popping her bubble gum like she's using it as punctuation. "Did those police buy your fake-ass story?"

"They did. Can't say I had much to tell them, or what's fake about it. I think I learned more from them than they did from me."

"That's my Superman! Do they know anything about Coco? Did they say if they have any suspects?"

"No. That wasn't the focus of our conversation. I don't think they're putting a whole lot of effort into Coco or Daphne."

They share a knowing look. Nobody with a badge would be going out of their way to find a killer of prostitutes. It was the perfect time for me to ask my next question.

"Ladies, were any other women killed in, say, the last six months?"

Shorty gives me a shrug. "Nah. Nothing until Daphne."

"Nobody went missing?"

Blondie drums her long yellow fingernails against her sculpted thighs. "Oh! Antoinette went missing, remember?" She grabs Shorty's hand, squeezes.

"Can you tell me about her?" I ask, trying to keep the eagerness out of my voice. After all, this is a human being I'm asking about, a real person, who, depending on what I'm about to hear next, likely met a terrible end.

Same as my daughter, same as my daughter.

Blondie says, "White girl, long brown hair, very stylish. Liked wearing evening gowns, as if she'd just come from a society ball or something."

Shorty retracts her hand back from Blondie's grip. "Wore lots of costume jewelry, too. Tiaras, strings of pearls, that kind of thing. Got lots of attention from the country club johns."

"How long ago did she disappear?" I ask.

"Five months maybe," says Shorty.

"You're sure?"

Blondie nods. "It happened right when that construction started."

"How can you be so sure?"

"Because that corner used to be our showroom. Then the scaffolding and walls went up, and we got bumped over here."

"And then she disappeared?"

"Pretty much. The first week we moved down here.

"Any idea who took her that last night?"

"Nope."

"You never saw or heard from her again?" I ask.

"Nope and nope," says Shorty.

Blondie looks away, tears in her eyes.

Chapter Thirty-one

My intuition tells me that the swampy, reedy land around the pond should be searched, possibly dredged. Likely, they would find a skeletal corpse posing in death. A second hit I get is to search the land of the construction site itself.

Two victims? Maybe, maybe.

These are the kinds of things a police investigation can do. So, without a police department underwriting my very expensive intuition, I'll sit on my hunch for now and share it with the right person later. The right person likely being Detective No-name.

Now, I'm standing beside the gate to the construction site, waiting for the parade of pickup trucks to go by. Minutes earlier, the shift ends with the ringing of a bell, and I'm reminded again of the dinosaur quitting whistle in *The Flintstones*.

Antoinette. Daphne. Coco. All Caucasian, tall, thin, and glamorous. The killer has a type. I hate to plug Lana into my formula, but she fits the model, too. Though she hadn't been a lady of the night. The aberration stands out and worries me.

Wrong place, wrong time, I think again.

Serial killers generally kill within their own race. So I was most likely looking for a Caucasian male, anywhere between the ages of forty to fifty. Which would place his age between twenty and thirty, back when Lana had been killed. I'd yet to see a construction worker here over the age of sixty. And my fleeting glimpse of the guy holding the hardhat in the park as I'd been driven off had only verified maybe his race and maybe his age. Maybe. Sadly, my eyes had gone straight to the hardhat tucked under his arm. When I'd looked up again, stunned, he'd been replaced by a half dozen faces. I'd replayed the scene in my head over and over again, but nothing but fuzziness is there. A fuzzy face. Fuzzy skin tone. Fuzzy hair color.

But a man. Yes, a man.

He'd been watching the police procession

—I was sure of that. He'd been grinning. Maybe, maybe. Did I make that up? How reliable was my memory now? I didn't know, I didn't know. Then I had seen something under his arm—the hardhat. When I looked up again... gone, gone, gone.

Breathe, good, good.

The gate opens and out comes the procession of mostly pick-up trucks. I look for the out-of-state tags that I'd jotted down with their makes and models. Two were pick-up trucks, one an SUV, and one a white Dodge Charger.

Within the first dozen vehicles I spot one of the plates from Idaho. It's the red Toyota Tacoma I'd noted in the crossword puzzle. The driver is a Hispanic male who falls within my estimated age range, forty to sixty. Not a perfect match—as he appears a bit darker than the fuzzy man in my memory, so I put an asterisk next to the license number.

Next, I spot the white Dodge Charger from California. The windows are tinted. It's impossible to see the driver. I put a question mark next to the license plate number on my list.

I bend my neck to see within the construction site. Some of the crew are lingering behind, enjoying a cold brewski in the long shadows of the late afternoon sunshine. My guy most likely isn't Joe six pack. My guy doesn't like too much socializing, I know this, feel this. It puts too many eyes and ears around his secretive and murderous ambitions.

Another out-of-state vehicle exits. It's a gold Chevy Tahoe from Oregon. The driver appears to be a white male in his mid-thirties. No gray anywhere to be seen. Hmm. By the time he's turned and accelerated up the street, I'm already wondering how to classify him. Is he another asterisk? My gut says he's not somebody who falls within the scope of my profile.

Now comes the last out-of-state vehicle. It's a black Ford F-150 from Idaho. The guy behind the wheel is white and in his late forties, gray in his beard. He's got a ponytail and noticeable acne. His eyes are shielded by a pair of Blue Blocker shades.

His license plate reads: Gunther.

I take a deep breath and watch him until he takes a turn toward the park. He's the only one to turn toward the park. On my crossword puzzle list, I circle his plate number.

Gunther.

Chapter Thirty-two

I lay in bed at the Eighth Avenue Shelter, my mind on Gunther from Idaho.

He falls within the age range, he's from out-of-state working in a transient industry, and he made a turn toward the park. His impulse to drive near his little acreage of horrors appears too alluring to resist. Which means he's probably driving the same route twice a day, to work and from work. Might even be taking trolls through the park, keeping an eye on his shallow burials.

Tailing him would be nice.

Slim and Benny are playing cards by the light of a dim wall sconce, huddled together at the edge of their cots. The room is sparsely populated, with maybe a half-dozen lumps all sawing logs.

I pull a folding chair over to the card game.

"Evening, gentlemen," I say, forcing a smile.

"Aloha." Slim winks at me with his green and yellow eye.

"Hullo," Benny mumbles.

"What're you boys playing?"

"Texas Hold 'em. Do you want in?"

They're using matchsticks for poker chips. "Do I need legal tender?"

"You got some." Slim shoves half his kitty to me. Benny scowls, aggrieved.

"Thank you for the generosity. Deal me in."

Benny is dealer. He gives me pocket queens and I raise pre-flop. The others limp in.

"You got bullets or blanks, Sheriff?"

I keep my eyes hooded as Benny lays out the flop. It's a rainbow of undercards. I still like my queens and push all-in.

"Jeezus Almighty," Benny whines.

"You best keep that Jesus stuff away from Miss Betty's ears," Slim warns. "She has the nature of a saint until someone uses His name in that way."

"Sorry, sorry."

Benny and Slim are both studying me.

"Why'd you call me Sheriff?" I ask.

"Just a term of respect. You came into the hand like a charging bull, like a new sheriff in town or something."

I nod, "I see."

Benny folds. Slim isn't done studying me.

"Why, Sheriff? Are you a real sheriff or something?"

"Ex-police."

Benny leans back like I might have a contagion. Slim nods and chuckles. "You have a quality about you, I guess. Knew you had an interesting story. What put you on the streets, bub?"

I can't determine if he's trying to get a read on my all-in or if he's genuinely interested. I remind myself that we're playing for matchsticks. "I lost my daughter. Murdered."

"Ah, sorry to hear it, guy," says Slim. "We didn't know."

I shrug. "No one did. I did my best to forget."

Slim folds his hand and exhales. "My amigo. My heart goes out to you."

"Very sorry for your loss, boss," Benny adds.

My cheeks are burning. Being the target of so much pity wasn't my reason for sitting down with them.

I rake in my pot. "I'm following a new lead

in the case."

That raises their eyebrows, and Slim pauses his shuffle.

"I have a suspect," I continue. "But he drives a vehicle and my crutches aren't going to keep up. Is there any way either of you know of that I can use to follow him?"

"Uber?" suggests Benny.

"Well, that's possible," says Slim. He deals the cards, but his mind is working on my problem. "But matchsticks aren't going to be enough. Do you know anyone with a credit card, guy? Or even a debit card or something?"

"I do, yes."

"Because that's legal tender for Uber. But it's going to get expensive. Like riding around in a taxi with the meter running."

My cards—a seven and nine of hearts—have soured like my mood.

"How about one of those electric scooters?" Benny says to Slim.

"Oh. The scooter. Brilliant, Benjamin." Slim antes up, looks at me. "Have you seen those scooters all around town? Green and black and motorized?"

"I trip over them every day." I can see the things, huddled together on every street corner in the city.

"But they require a credit card as well, my

friend. And they're none too fast, either. But you can find them everywhere and you can drive them yourself. Again, credit card."

Credit card, credit card, credit card.

How does a homeless man with just a few dollars and matchsticks to his name get a credit card? Slim asked if I knew someone, and I did. Oh, yes. I did.

My heart and my head swell with newfound hope. I can see the next part of the investigation ahead of me like a wide open highway. I ante up. Suddenly, I like my hand.

Chapter Thirty-three

It's before dawn and I'm seated at a bus stop bench just outside the park's main entrance.

I'm not bothering with the construction site any longer. This is the new leading edge of my investigation, trying to determine from which direction he approaches the park. That will help lay out my next line of focus: Tailing him back to his lair. No matter how many morning and evening commutes, no matter how many scooter rentals, I'm going to find where this guy is shacking up.

The street is quiet now, but getting busier with the rising sun.

The freeway on- and off-ramps are to my

left. If Gunther comes from that direction, it's going to greatly impact how effective and expeditious my series of tails are going to play out. I'm hoping he comes from my right, the south. That would indicate he's more local. Maybe staying in one of the fleabag rooms or roach motels near the wharfs.

As the morning sky brightens, the nearby streets fill up with morning commuters. The bus lines and light rail buzz with activity. I don't miss the morning commutes to the precinct. The bumper-to-bumper traffic, the desperate red-light racers, the aggressive lane changers, the little convoys of speeders all thinking there's safety in numbers...

Oh, shit. Wow.

There he is. Inbound from the south. I'm so hyper-focused, I begin doubting it's really him. Maybe it's just a lookalike black F-150. But sure enough, Gunther is slowing to make a left turn into the park. He's not wearing his Blue Blockers and I can see his eyes clearly. They look mud black, set close together and pinched, like he's trying to recall what his last victim sounded like as he lorded over her final breaths.

He makes the turn, passes in front of me. No surprise: his mud flaps have the pole dancer silhouettes.

I turn in my seat, watch him cruise through

the park. He pauses near the pond. Too far to see him now. A minute later he's moving again, toward a side exit, and now he's gone.

Wow, what a fucking creep.

Deep, breath, good, good.

And fuck him.

Chapter Thirty-four

I head over to Annie's RV and take a perch on her bump-out step, waiting for any sign of wakefulness. After an hour or so I can hear the suspension squeak and fluid going into the commode as Annie relieves her bladder.

I give her another ten minutes, rap on the door.

"Hey, handsome," she says at the open door. I half expected her to be in a floral bathrobe and hair curlers. But it's a blue flannel shirt and gray sweat pants. She beckons me in.

I climb up and duck inside. Coffee is on. Her little TV is tuned to Fox News.

"Can I get you some coffee?" she asks.

She motioned toward the kitchenette table,

where I sit. "Thank you. Yes."

She grabs a coffee cup and saucer from the drying rack, looks over her shoulder. "You look good."

"Thanks to you."

"Yeah, but you still look good. Could have gone to hell by now. How you feeling up here?" She taps her temple with her forefinger as she pours coffee.

"Sharp."

"Sharp?" She chuckles, returns the carafe to its niche. "Sounds like police speak."

"Guilty as charged," I say.

"You any closer to finding whoever did a number on you?"

"Yes."

"You ever going to tell me what happened?"

"Someday. I have a favor to ask."

She picks up a remote control and turns down the TV's volume. "Ask away."

"I need to get around town, and quickly, but the only viable method to use are those little rental scooters."

"The scourge of the city."

"They require a debit card."

She nods, understanding. "I can provide you with one."

I rub my neck, overwhelmed again by her

generosity. "I can't pay you back right away."

She waves a hand, dismissing the thought. "What else do you need, handsome?"

"Can I take another shave and shower?"

She chuckles. "Being clean gets habit-forming, doesn't it? How about a fresh set of clothes?"

"You're reading my mind."

She provides me with another yellow towel and wash rag. "Use the razor from last time. On the sink still. There's a bar of soap or liquid in the shower caddy, pick your poison."

I leave my crutches at the table and maneuver into the little bathroom. Though it's cramped, it's ideally spaced for someone with a gimpy foot: it's impossible to lose your balance and fall when you're in a phone booth.

As I lather up my face, looking myself in the mirror, the world suddenly goes dim and my mind trips.

Where am I? Who am I? *Where? Who?*

My head and thoughts spin and I brace myself against the wall before lowering myself onto the toilet seat.

"What kind of attire are you looking for?" someone asks from beyond the door. "Khakis again? Business casual?"

Who is that? What's business casual?

I squeeze my eyes shut, blocking out light

and sound, breathing deep and deliberate.

"Are you alright in there, fella?"

I blink and hear the words replaying in my mind, over and over: breathe, relax, good good.

Breathe, relax, good good. I do just that and shake my head.

"Yes," I say, standing again. I'm in Annie's RV about to shave and shower. Yes, good good.

"Khakis work," I say. I'm still not sure what the hell business casual is.

I stare at my reflection. A moment ago my face was that of a stranger's. Now it's back to being mine.

I'm back, back...

Back.

Chapter Thirty-five

I step out of the RV and into the blinding light of day.

Scanning the street, I spot my target: an electric scooter propped up at a nearby street corner.

I'm wearing khakis, a baby blue button-down shirt, dark brown loafers and matching suspenders. The crutches are too heavy and cumbersome for the scooter, so I'm venturing out with only a retractable walking cane, courtesy of Annie.

Annie, Annie, sweet Annie.

I hobble to the scooter, hoping like hell someone doesn't nab it before I do. No one does, and now I'm reading the instructions on how to activate the damned thing.

Not damned, no, no, no.

A gift from God, surely.

The scooter is blue and black, the name *Seagull* stamped onto its foot deck. I swipe the credit card, and follow more instructions. Miracle of miracles, the card works, and the scooter is ready for me.

Thank you, God. Thank you, thank you.

I step aboard with my good foot, steadying myself with the cane. Once my bad foot is steady, I fold the cane and shove it in my back pocket. Both hands on the handlebar grips. Steady, steady good. I press the thumb-throttle. The motor engages, and I twist the handle toward me slowly, slowly... and now I'm moving forward. Shaky at first, uncertain. I remind myself to only hop down on my good foot, should I suddenly need to. Hopping down on my bad foot will likely cause me to break it all over again.

I navigate the contours of the sidewalk and crosswalks, trying to find a comfortable cruising speed. I need to move fast enough to stay upright, but slow enough to avoid obstacles and pedestrians. I find myself staring directly at the pavement in my path. Tunnel vision must be a beginner's habit. I know I should be more aware of my surroundings, scanning for oncoming threats, but I don't trust my driving skills yet.

I reach a busy intersection and brake. My good foot steps down to the pavement as I wait for the crosswalk.

My bad foot is already throbbing. The deformity, over the years, has atrophied all of the little muscle flexors that are used to help stabilize a foot. Now my foot and ankle's long-dormant muscle flexors are being asked to keep my foot steady on a narrow platform that's constantly changing pitch and direction. It's a glaring hole in my scooter forethought. How did I miss this key problem in the planning stage? It's not too late to abort the scooter and try acquiring, say, a bicycle. But that would bring its own slew of complications.

The crosswalk blinks and I motor across the street. I next make a concerted effort to keep my eyes up and on swivels, so to speak. I notice scooters everywhere. Parked in bunches on every street corner. Being ridden on every patch of pavement in the city. Some riders are in business casual, like myself, while others are in grungy flannel skinny jeans. The largest contingent of the scooter population is teenagers, cannonballing down sidewalks and curbsides with a fearlessness that's, admittedly, contagious.

I decide to open up the throttle. The little LED speedometer on the handlebars begins to climb, eventually topping out at 15.6 MPH.

I'm not going to lie: at top speed, the ride is thrilling. My face is fixed into a smear of exhilaration and panic. As I begin weaving through some foot traffic, it occurs to me that I'm one bad turn away from a wipeout that will undoubtedly result in a painful scrape along the sidewalk and some broken bones.

Good, maybe they can fix my ankle.

Maybe, but the killer will be long gone by then.

With that thought, I ease off the throttle and steer toward the park. It's time to begin the groundwork for tailing Gunther.

Chapter Thirty-six

I reach the park's entryway, then travel the empty sidewalk down to where Gunther's vehicle had paused by the pond this morning.

I'm the only sidewalk traffic along this stretch. The afternoon sun is blocked by the park's tree line of poplar and spruce, casting a cold shadow. The wind is picking up. I regret not including a jacket with my ensemble.

It is early still. Quitting time is another half hour away. I study the pond, the tall grass, the reeds, and wonder where his other victims are. They're out there, perhaps close by, perhaps on the other side of the pond. Either way, messy work with the sludge and mud. Too messy for a guy with a bum ankle.

I turn around and head back up to the park's entrance, turn left, and settle in at a four way intersection that will give me views of both the construction site and a clear idea which direction Gunther will head off to. If his pattern holds, if he swings by the park after work. He will. I know it. He has to.

Has to, has to!

I breathe, focus, breathe.

To the south is a bustling shopping district. From there, I know the road veers southeast toward the city's wharf and through a section of urban blight in desperate need of a wrecking ball. If I had to hazard a guess which direction Gunther will go after quitting time, easy money is straight through the intersection toward the wharf. There's cheap room and board in the industrial zone along the railroad yards.

I take a seat on the nearest bus stop bench and watch for him.

My mind drifts back to my relapse in the shower. It's got me stirred up for some reason. Sanity, to me, feels like a hot-air balloon caught between mountain peaks below and storm clouds above. Only a very narrow window will keep me from crashing back down or succumbing to the turbulence above. Either way, annihilation surrounds me.

A half hour later, through half-closed lids, I

notice a black F-150 coming up the busy street from the direction of the construction site. My eyes widen a little. This isn't the first black F-150, after all. Hell, not the first in the last five minutes. It switches into the left turn lane into the park. I reach out and take hold of the scooter's black grip.

Blinker on like a good boy—the truck is turning into the park.

I get the scooter underway, moving at full-speed toward the same park entrance, but he's got a jump on me, and I lose sight of him. I reach the entryway and scan. The parking area is a chain of lots that winds all the way back to the duck pond. His truck is nowhere in sight.

Where, where?

I rocket down the sidewalk, down to the big fountain. The park is notably empty. The weather is turning rotten, heavy storm clouds amassing to the northwest. I decide to forget the parking lots and take the paved running trail that winds back toward my favorite bench.

I round a bend... and catch sight of Gunther standing on the exact spot where I found Daphne's body. He's bigger than I expected. About six-foot-three, 250 lbs. Tree trunk neck, barrel chest, and pot belly. Wearing a sweaty ensemble of patchwork jeans, long-sleeve thermal with Day Glo vest, and black skullcap.

Gray stubble on his cheeks and chin and neck.

I reach into my pants pocket, grip the small pistol there. One shot.

Call the police. Call Detective Hunan. Call anyone.

No, no, no. It's him, him, him.

The killer. I know it, he knows it, God knows it.

I maintain my speed and direction, trying to appear like a regular park-goer in business casual attire on a rented scooter. The scooter won't work on the grass; at least, I don't think. Maybe the smoother patches. Would take me fifteen minutes to hobble to him. No element of surprise. He would see me coming a mile away.

What to do, what to do?

Meanwhile, I roll out of sight, around a curve in the little park street that meanders from parking lot to parking lot. At the edge of the duck pond I pause and count to thirty. If I head back too quickly, it might appear suspicious. If I wait too long, he might get back in his truck and vanish, delaying my tail and wasting an entire day of rental fees. (My intention is to keep track of my scooter charges and eventually pay Annie back.)

I turn around and head back the way I came. As I round the tree line, I see he's gone, and just catch the bastard exiting the park. I ease back on the throttle and watch him head south, toward the wharf, toward the cheap housing. At least he's driving away from the red-light district. No killing tonight.

It was him, him, him.

I know it. Felt it.

Still feel it. In fact, I step off the scooter and sit right there and bury my face in my hands.

Chapter Thirty-seven

It is Thursday evening, and I approach Grace Hunan's house on the electric scooter.

Although I know she's not at the window awaiting my arrival—she might've forgotten all about our dinner date—I'm feeling self-conscious about riding up to her place on a rented electric scooter. I considered tucking it behind her neighbor's tree. But I'd vowed last time to not bother with false fronts. Grace possesses a non-judgmental integrity that inspires me to boldly drive the scooter right up to her front steps and park. I hobble to the door and ring the bell.

Our date was one of the reasons I wanted to get cleaned up earlier today. Okay, the main reason.

Nervous, nervous, breathe, breathe.

As she opens, I see that her hands are occupied with a dish towel. "Right on time, James. Glad you could make it." She stands to the side, offering a welcoming smile.

"Home-cooked meal and good company. Sounds like heaven."

It's also the first social outing I've had in decades. With that in mind, I present her with a single red rose that's been stashed in my shirt for the last three miles. Thorns have been poking me the whole time.

"Thank you, James! I see you haven't forgotten how to charm the hostess."

She leads me to the kitchen. It's a chef's wonderland, every appliance imaginable, including a pasta maker. There's a salad bowl with hearts of romaine. On her cutting board are onion and tomato. On the table is a setting for two, including a bottle of red wine. And lastly, next to the wine, is a collection of files piled high enough to be leaning.

I'm not sure if it's the aroma of lasagna baking in the oven, or Grace's natural warmth, but my mouth is salivating.

"Would you like to have a seat?" she asks, opening a cupboard and removing a slender glass vase, which she fills with water at the sink. She slips the single rose within and sets the whole thing in the center of the table. The whole process is so effortless I get the impression that her late husband had given her a lifetime of flowers. Good, she deserved them.

I take a seat between the wine bottle and stack of files.

"I wasn't sure whether you would be interested in wine. Feel free to open it or ignore it."

The prospect of wine is intriguing, and I fumble with the cork and opener until I subdue the former. Don Juan I am not. Well, at least not these days. I pour out two glasses, and set the wine on the table.

"And please make yourself comfortable, dig into the case if you're ready. You must be dying with anticipation. We can make this a working dinner."

She's so intuitive it's humbling. I begin sorting through the materials, subconsciously putting the folders into three piles: Must-see, promising, and cursory.

"Some things are missing," she says. "Specifically, some suspect profiles that we'd worked up. A couple guys I really felt strongly about. But the evidence was highly circumstantial…" She pulls the lasagna hot from the oven.

"Does the name Gunther ring any bells?"

"Now you're putting a lot of strain on an old detective's memory." She places the steaming cookware on a hot pad near my triage of file folders. "I don't remember a Gunther. First name or surname?"

"Not sure."

She serves me a plate of authentic Italian cuisine. I push the case files aside and breathe in the rich tomato sauce and sharp Parmesan. The first bite is like the pancakes that morning at Finley's: a forkful of heaven.

She reads my face and giggles. "That bad?"

"That good. Is it a family recipe?"

More giggling. "Naw, just a quick Google search."

"Google?"

"Oh." She touches my shoulder. "Sorry, James. Sometimes I take for granted the things you might've missed. Google is a—"

"I'm kidding, Grace. I know what Google is."

My joke catches her off guard and she laughs so suddenly that her latest forkful of lasagna drops in her wine glass. This makes her laugh even more. A laughter that turns into a squeal. She covers her mouth, embarrassed and delighted at the same time.

"That was all your fault," she says, using

her fork to dig out the lost bite.

"I take full responsibility. Isn't that what a good dinner-guest does?"

"Indeed it is. The hostess is *never* the perpetrator of such a faux pas."

"The faux pas was entirely mine. Obviously, I'm rusty at these things. By these things, I mean actual human conversation. I apologize."

"Apology accepted, and you're doing great James."

With the lasagna successfully speared on one end of the fork, she laughingly offers it to me, of which I surprise the hell out of her and chomp down, sliding the wine-marinated bite into my own mouth. She squeals again and slaps my arm.

"I was just kidding, James! It must have tasted terrible."

"It was delicious, and when you're from the streets you never kid about food. Or waste it."

Her hand lingers on my arm, and soon we eat in bemused silence as I scan a folder containing a timeline that details the case's various threads and emergent leads. The last entry is dated January 14, 2000.

"Nothing significantly new, I'm afraid," she says.

I continue through the must-see pile and pause on the rape kit's analysis. Semen was acquired and a DNA profile was run. No matches were found in the state database.

"Was the DNA sample ever run against the national database?"

"No. It wasn't readily available at that time."

"So the last time it was ever analyzed was 1999?"

"Yes."

I come across some photos taken post mortem. Color close-ups of Lana's bruised and bloodied body. A small ruler in the pictures helps to establish context. They're images no father should have to see of his daughter.

"I think I'll have more wine. A lot more."

Grace silently uncorks it and pours generously. I take a slug or three.

After a few long moments, I say, "There've been some new deaths that I believe are related to Lana's case. All in the last six months. And all prostitutes working in proximity to where my chief suspect is working."

"Would that be Gunther?"

"It would."

"And would the prostitutes include Coco and Daphne?"

"And another named Antoinette. How'd you know?"

"I had a conversation earlier today with

Detective Schulte."

I freeze, fork halfway to my lips. "What's Schulte's first name?"

"Jennifer."

"Blond, green eyes?"

"Yes."

Ah, I've got a name to the face now. Curiously, I'd been watching that park for days and hadn't seen a single unmarked. No police presence whatsoever. I knew the precinct had other pressing matters to deal with. I also knew the political machinations that tied detectives' hands. Mostly, I knew that some victims just didn't rate too high. They had a legit serial killer in the presence... and still the files were pushed to the side.

"Tell me more about Gunther," says Grace.

"Sure. He works at the construction site downtown at the corner of Richly and Beemer. Some high-rise that I believe is going to be condos. I think he's a welder. Big guy, probably six-three and 260. Age forty-five to fifty-five. Gray hair in a ponytail."

"Why don't I pass this along to Schulte?"

"No. Not yet." I sit back, try to decompress. Head spinning. From the wine? I don't know, I don't know.

"You shouldn't be doing this alone, James."

I look at her. "I... have you."

She smiles. "You do, James. Anything to catch this guy."

"Then I suggest the first order of business is to run the DNA through the state and federal systems. And to get this plate checked." I reach inside my back pocket and remove the folded piece of newspaper. I push the crossword puzzle across the table.

She smiles. "Consider it done."

Chapter Thirty-eight

It's after midnight.

We've gone through everything on Lana, analyzing each file's relevance to my current activities. Since I know so little about Gunther, we can't determine whether anything we're looking at is implicating or exonerating him. That he's involved in the current slate of murders, I have no doubt. Whether or not he killed my Lana, I don't yet know.

Soon, I think. *Soon, soon.*

We also talk at length about personal and professional matters: our former significant others, our long-gone careers, our future hopes and aspirations. The more I get to know her, the more I'm drawn to her. She's an exceptional woman. Smart and caring and giving. As we wrap up, there's an awkward moment at the kitchen table when conversation stalls out. I don't want to leave, but we've reached the part of the night where I either put my feelings on the table and try staying overnight, or I push my feelings down into the castle vault and act as if my intention all along was to depart at the conclusion of our dinner date.

"Thank you for the lasagna."

"Would you like some for the road?"

"I'd love leftovers, but my mode of transportation isn't equipped for cargo."

"Would you like me to give you a ride someplace?"

"No. I wouldn't want to inconvenience you."

"James... I'm not inconvenienced. It's late. The scooter isn't safe or reliable at any time of day, let alone midnight."

"I'm staying at the Eighth Avenue Shelter. That's downtown near the corner of Eighth and Rosewood."

"Then that's where you're getting dropped off. I'll get my keys."

Okay, shoot. Things hadn't gone the way I'd hoped. She gave no opening to the possibility of my staying. Had I sensed something that wasn't really there? Was I reading between lines that hadn't been written in the first place?

She packs the rest of the lasagna in a plastic container and I load the scooter into the back of her SUV, and we hit the road. Headlights wash over the quiet street. A steady rain begins.

"There's something I'm not clear on, James…"

Here it comes. Time for us to discuss *us*. Better late than never.

"How do you connect Gunther to Lana? The missing tooth isn't corroborating enough to establish a link. Lots of killers take trophies. And as far as I know, she wasn't a prostitute." She adds this last part gently.

Whoops. I misread the tea leaves again. We're just talking shop.

"She was a college student. He might have been too, or recently graduated. More than likely, he trolled the college party scene."Grace nods. She knows the case. "She was coming home from a party. Gunther, would have likely been in his early twenties."

"Better looking, in shape," I added.

"Easier to pick up women," says Grace. "Now he's older, heavier, and his M.O. changes with time. Quite simply, hookers are easier to pick up, and their deaths or disappearances aren't as heavily investigated. The Green River Killer murdered hundreds, or so he says."

Running the plate would give us a lot of this information: the name of the registered owner, his age, address, and past addresses. Once we had that, we could nail down Gunther's whereabouts at the time of Lana's death. Likely, he had just moved to the area. Likely, Lana had been one of his first victims. The good news is, Grace was going to head out to the station tomorrow morning to see about running that plate. Also, she was going to look into running the DNA from Lana's rape kit. The plate and DNA could be a match. If so, that should be enough to arrest the bastard. And then what, a lengthy trial? Or, worse, prosecutors brokering a deal with the bastard: you tell us where the other victims are, and we spare your life.

I begin rocking a little in my seat. Grace glances over at me, noticing.

"Is this too much, James? Should we change the subject?"

"It's okay, it's okay."

We're passing through a dark patch of the city. The dashboard lights illuminate her delicate face. Brows wrinkled, eyes flitting between me and the road. Something is bothering her. My behavior? The case? A little of both.

"I'll admit, this theory you have on Gunther

is more complete than what I thought you had. But that doesn't answer the bigger picture."

"What bigger picture?"

Were we going to finally discuss us? Or was she going to pull another Lucy and yank the football out of my way again?

"If these leads have any merit, which they very possibly might, then why are you endangering yourself and the investigation by following Gunther?"

My head starts to throb. I look down at my lap. There's a plastic container with something inside. Curious, I lift the lid. It smells like food.

"James. Are you alright?"

I frown, wondering where I am. Some kind of vehicle, yes. Outside, the blur of scenery is too dark to recognize. The vehicle is slowing down…

"I'm getting concerned, James. What's happening?"

The voice sounds familiar, but it also sounds like it's coming from beyond a crashing waterfall. A hand reaches through the cascading barrier and, grips my wrist.

I shriek as I fumble with the door handle. There are two things I must do right now—two musts to accomplish: get out of the vehicle and not drop the container of food. Every thought and action are focused on these two musts.

"James! Please don't open the door!"

I pull the handle, kick the door open. The hand now grabs at my shoulder.

"No!" I rip my shoulder away and bail out of the vehicle, hitting the wet ground hard, rolling, rolling, crashing up against a curb heavy with rain water. I push myself up. A black SUV has screeched to a halt a few feet away. A door is opening.

I find my feet. One of them is broken. Or had been broken, I don't remember, I don't remember.

And now I'm across a sidewalk, over a metal rail, and stumbling down a hillside next to the road, down, down...

Chapter Thirty-nine

I awaken with droplets hitting my forehead.

It's dark and I'm soaked to the bone and lying on a very familiar surface: the park bench. To me it's like a lumpy mattress, my body perfectly melding to its fiberglass slats. Something is clutched in my hand. It's a box of some sort. I turn it over, trying to solve the puzzle. What's inside the box?

I crack the lid. It's food. I'm hungry. I shovel the cold pasta and tomato sauce into my mouth, chewing just long enough to work the bites down my esophagus. Esophagus. What a strange term. The cold pasta and tomato sauce are going down my *esophagus*…

Strange, strange.

The rain is picking up. I can't stay out in this rain without my coat. Where's my coat? I had a coat with a hood. Now I'm wearing some kind of fancy pants with *suspenders*. I've never worn suspenders. I'm not even sure I'm saying the word correctly. Suspenders. A stupid name for a useless piece of clothing.

I need to find a coat. Something, anything to keep me warm and dry.

How did I end up on the park bench wearing suspenders and holding a plastic box of cold pasta?

Lasagna.

Grace!

Her face swims into view. So does her SUV. We were talking, talking, then came the crashing water, and pain, lots of pain. A memory of rolling? Down a hill? Maybe, maybe. Then walking and whimpering and now I'm here, shivering, hands bleeding. Knees bleeding. Ankle screaming.

I get to my feet, or try to. I stumble, stumble. Water is pressing between my toes, my shoes are acting like sponges. I don't have my crutches… how could I be so dumb that I'm wearing suspenders and fancy shoes that absorb water instead of shielding it? No coat. No crutches.

Grace. I was trying to be something I

J.R. RAIN

couldn't. Trying to forge a relationship which I'm not equipped to have.

I know what I need to do. I didn't crawl out from under the rock because I wanted to find romance. I crawled out from under the rock to find a killer.

I blink and the buzzing at the back of my mind dissipates. Good, good. Breathe, relax.

So cold. I know, I know.

The words "debit card" appear in my thoughts, and I thrust my hands into my front pockets. There, there, there! A plan forms, wavers, disappears, forms again.

I start walking, my twisted foot making every step excruciating.

Excruciating. What a strange word.

To my amazement, I find a fold-out cane in my back pocket.

I unfold it, lean on it.

Thank you, God.

Thank you!

206

Chapter Forty

I arrive at a 24-hour Walmart, the first step in the plan.

I find the aisle of art supplies, select a medium-tip Sharpie, and then draw a black arrow on the back of each of my hands that points upward toward my elbows. I roll up the sleeves of my shirt and begin scrawling the following text on my left forearm: *Gunther. Works construction at corner of Richly and Beemer. Staying most likely by the wharf. Black Ford F-150. License plate: GUNTHER.*

Since I don't know when my next mental breakdown will occur, I can't afford to take any chances. Leaving a trail of reminders will hopefully keep me from losing my way. It's not a sure-fire strategy, but it's all I have at the moment.

In the men's clothing department I select black cargo pants with plenty of pockets. A black zip-up hoodie. Black ball-cap. Black sneakers.

I next hit the home improvement section and begin selecting my tools: an 18-ounce hammer with a flex claw, some black duct tape.

Why did both breakdowns occur when I was with my most trusted friends and confidants? Of all the people I've interacted with over the last few days, why would my mind fail me *only* when I was with Annie and Grace? It's a question that gnaws at me. A painful reminder that nobody can keep me tethered to this world. And if I'm slowly losing that tether and have a limited window in which to act, then I need to finish my business as soon as possible.

Now, now!

In the sporting goods section, I pick out a seven-inch tactical flashlight with telescoping lens and a nine-inch Bowie Knife with teeth notched along its spine.

The bicycles run anywhere from $80.00 to $500.00. I pick out a mountain bike for $190.00. It's sturdy enough for my needs. Limping, I wheel the shopping cart and mountain bike to the lone cashier. The young woman has several nose piercings. Her nametag says "Claudia."

As I place my purchases on the moving belt, the pattern of what they represent becomes startlingly apparent to me. The stuff I'm buying, separately, are just an assortment of clothes and tools and transportation. But bought all together, they tell a story. And that story would clearly be that I'm going to stealthily incapacitate and harm somebody.

And since that's exactly why I'm buying all of this gear, it makes me wonder whether or not Claudia is pressing some button under the counter, secretly alerting the manager or authorities.

I'm watching her face for a reaction, but she stays impassive as she rings me up.

Still, it's the middle of the night and I'm getting paranoid that my purchases are getting flagged. I make a visual sweep, looking for other employees and nearby security cameras. But nobody else is around and the cameras are all tucked behind those dark domes hanging from the rafters.

I realize my forearms are still uncovered, with the black words scrawled up and down my flesh. I don't know if Claudia has noticed. I casually lower my arms out of view and roll down my shirtsleeves.

"Your total will be $313.14."

I pull the debit card from my shirt pocket. If Claudia's going to check the name on it, my shopping spree is most likely over. But Claudia doesn't check. I finish the transaction—using the PIN code provided by Annie—collect my belongings and receipt, and wheel my Gunther-hunting kit out of the store.

Outside, I glance around for any police response. But there aren't any squad cars with flashers and nobody's waiting to question or cuff me. Claudia either failed to see me for what I am or simply didn't care. I step into the shadows of the garden department's exterior and roll up my right sleeve.

I use the Sharpie to add some new words: *Go to wharf. Find black F-150. License plate: GUNTHER.*

Chapter Forty-one

My club foot doesn't want to play nice with the bicycle pedal, and keeps sliding off.

I pull the black duct tape from one of my cargo pockets, rip off a lengthy piece, and wrap my foot snug to the pedal. Crisis solved. Duct tape really is a universal fix-all.

I get the bike up to speed and the night air feels good on my face. There's the familiar smell of forbidden adventure and pleasure that only the night air can stoke. An almost arousing sensation that entices your imagination, hinting that something illicit or intoxicating or dangerous can be found around every dark corner if you're willing to brave it.

Thinking clear, feeling good.

But now I represent that illicitness. I'm the agent of danger. If anybody was to blunder across my path tonight, be it the police or a curious bystander, they'd be intervening in my very thorny business. Things could take a nasty turn for all involved, so I pray I'm ignored.

A new note is added to the night air: the sea. The familiar scent of fish and brine and salt and sand. A familiar scent that invokes memories of another life and time. Immediately I'm picturing Lana as a toddler, wearing a bright yellow bathing suit with inflated orange floaties on her upper arms. She can't lower her arms to her sides and is growing frustrated, but my wife is adamant that she keep the inflatables on.

To take her mind off the obstructions, I pick her up and carry her over the ocean's edge, balancing her so that she's flying. She knows the drill and giggles. Arms outstretched, she zooms over the knee-deep waves. I can feel her little Buddha belly quiver with laughter and delight.

The sidewalk ripples and the sky above spins. I gasp. The handlebars wobble in my arms. There's a bend in the sidewalk coming up, I know it and had prepared for it. Too late, too late. My front tire hits a low brick wall, and I flip over the handlebars. The bike flips with me. I tumble through the hedgerow with the bike still attached to my foot. Every exposed patch of skin raked over by hundreds of little nettles. The bike and I end up half tangled in the brush and half sprawled on the sidewalk. My leg is aflame, twisted and cockeyed.

Gasping, I strip the tape off. My leg might be fractured. In the least, my knee is torn or sprained. I crawl out of the hedgerow, and vomit from the pain. Up comes the lasagna.

I turn away from the contents of my stomach and roll onto my back. A full moon stares down, its pale cold light touching every-where. A false light, a reflection only. But light nonetheless, doing its best before the sun rises and snuffs it out.

I feel the sun rising on me too. Except it's not the sun. It's insanity.

Why am I wearing black? Why was I taped to a bicycle?

My pants pockets are weighed down with stuff. I dig out a hammer, hunting knife, and flashlight. What was I going to do with these? The fright I'm feeling is so profound I'm paralyzed—blanking about where I was going or who I was going to visit.

In the pale light, I see something written on my hand. An arrow, pointing up my arm. I push up my sleeve.

Go to wharf. Find black F-150. Idaho

plate: GUNTHER.

I check my other arm: *Gunther. Works construction at corner of Richly and Beemer. Stays most likely by the wharf.*

Flashing memories crash back like a storm surge. I get the bike back upright. The frame is intact and the wheels check out. I climb back on and start to pedal. My foot slips off, again and again. My knee, my God my knee. Tears squeeze free, roll down my cheeks.

Duct tape, duct tape!

I find it in my pockets, re-tape my foot, grunting and crying out from the pain in my knee and ankle. Once done, I fish out the black Sharpie from a zippered pocket and write lower on my left arm. After all, I know what's triggering my fade-out spells. I write:

No love, no happiness, no memories.
Just get the job done.

Chapter Forty-two

It's just after 3 a.m. when I find his truck.

It's at a roadside fleabag called The Seaward Motel. Two floors, each with a row of fifteen rooms. The center of the parking lot is a fenced-in swimming pool that's dark and lifeless. The truck is parked midway along the stretch of rooms. I'm guessing he's in unit 106 or 107. If he was upstairs, he would've parked next to one of the two staircases rather than midway between them.

My leg is a wildfire. I know I should be seeking medical care. Or just ice and elevate. But I'm too close to Gunther. At this point, my leg is collateral damage. I'm willing to accept that.

I slip the bike behind the corner of the building and check the message on my left forearm: *No love, no happiness, no memories.*

I repeat it to myself. Thoughts and memories of lovely little Lana are strictly forbidden. Instead, I picture her in the police photos. The bruising, the tearing, the cold pale form that was the leftovers of lovely little Lana.

I hobble toward 106 and 107. I can feel the weight of the hammer in my left cargo pocket bouncing against my thigh. My right hand is gripping the handle of the Bowie Knife in my right cargo pocket. The gun is in another pocket. I don't want the gun, not unless I need it. It's good that it's there, though. Metal courage.

I reach the pair of rooms and peek through the window of 106, but the curtains are closed. I look into 107. The curtains are open. The room is unoccupied. I turn my full attention to 106. He's on the other side of this door. I'd be lying if I said I wasn't scared and excited and exhilarated. I curl my fingers into a fist and get ready to rap on the door, but I pause…

The parking lot has seven other vehicles, including a dented red Honda Civic one space away from the truck. It could belong to the occupant of 106. This is a complication. If I knock, or try gaining entry with my tools, I might find someone other than Gunther.

I lower my hand. This isn't the right approach. I should wait him out. Let him reveal himself. I slip into the pool area and take a seat in one of the sunning chairs. I pull my hood over my head, rub my arms for warmth, and watch...

Chapter Forty-three

I'm the boy with the thick black cowlick and overalls, running barefoot through a sunny field of wild yellow mustard flowers. The smell of sweet clover surrounds me. Everything feels clean and healthy and alive.

I'm approaching a narrow and winding brook. A weeping willow tree stands in an ox-bow bend, its lush umbrella of branches acting like a curtain. I reach for the branches and separate them. Lana is waiting in the shade. She's just a little girl. I smile at her. She smiles back at me, but she's missing a front tooth. I don't think much of it because I'm also missing a front tooth. That's because we're both kids. Like her, I'm not much older than seven or eight.

But *her* missing front tooth is a bloody crater. Her eyes widen as a shadow falls over the willow branches. I step in front of her. I want to protect her, but I'm so little, so weak.

The shadow stretches larger, blocking out the sun altogether. I try clasping Lana's fingers in mine but I only clasp cold air. I turn back, but she's gone.

The black shadow falls over me, obliterating all light and air...

I awake, screaming—or trying to scream. Something over my head, something's suffocating me—*it's a plastic bag, a plastic bag!*

Instead of inhaling air I'm drawing the plastic into my throat. I try flailing and fighting off the plastic but I can't breathe, can't breathe, can't breathe. Thoughts deadening. Body feeling limp. I'm back in the hole, the peaceful hole...

Just get the job done.

The knife, the knife. Is that my hand searching for it? Maybe, maybe.

There, got it. A surge of energy. I slash up into the bag, narrowly missing my face. Air washes over me, sweet air. My other hand—somehow brandishing the hammer—swinging in a looping uppercut behind my back. I feel the weight of my attacker retreat. I roll off the chair and onto the ground. Gunther is holding the shreds of a plastic bag, bleeding from a gash in his right forearm.

I kneel at the pool's edge, sucking in air.

He kicks the chair aside and feints toward me but I instantly slash out with both weapons, aiming for his knees. He stays safely out of my range and pulls a gun. It looks like a standard Glock.

"Who are you?" he asks.

I take a wheezy inhale, say nothing.

His eyes are deep set and shrouded in shadow; mouth and chin are set in a grim smile. "Drop your knife and hammer in the pool." He points his gun over my head. "Then we'll go into my room and finish this conversation in private."

I don't drop my weapons.

"Drop them."

I set them on the pool deck.

"Stand and walk."

"No."

He's stuck and he knows it. A gunshot will draw too much attention. He's lived a life in the shadows, killing in the shadows, too. "What do you think you know, old man?"

"I know you've killed at least three women."

He stares at me. "You were at the park.

How long have you been following me?"

"Long enough to know who you are and what you did."

"And what did I do?"

"Killed my daughter."

"I've killed lots of daughters, old man." He snaps his fingers. "The college student, here in Seattle. One of my first. Yes, yes. Learned to stay away from the good girls after that one. They draw way, *way* too much attention. The bad girls not so much."

My hands shake. I try to breathe.

"Why do you keep looking to the side, old man?"

It's an old trick I learned. I smile, or try to. "Maybe because there's someone behind you."

He pauses. A hint of doubt on his face.

I reach for the gun in my pocket. Which pocket, which pocket? There, found it, found it! He fires his own, hitting me in the chest. I expected that. I raise my gun, or try to. He shoots again, this time in my stomach. Another hits my shoulder. A fourth shot misses entirely.

I raise my hand and fire the single shot from the Cobra Derringer. As I collapse, I see him go down too. Good, good...

I'm my little self again, with a missing tooth, back on the bank of the babbling brook, crouching in the sun-dappled shadows of the willow trees. The air still has that heavenly aroma of—

Yanked back into the pale cold light of police flashers and screaming sirens of first responders. Yelling, pounding feet. Blinding flashlight beams in my eyes. Several faces appear in and out of my view. I recognize one of them. Detective No-Name. Yes, she has a name but I can't remember it, not now. It's okay that I can't remember.

"Hello, James. How're you feeling?" she asks.

I can't move or speak. Her smile falters.

Now I'm in an ambulance. Someone is holding my hand.

Grace. She's crying.

I squeeze her hand.

Or try to.

Chapter Forty-four

I'm back under the willow tree. Back in my overalls and boyish cowlick. Lovely little Lana is at my side. We're searching the ground for something.

"Goodbye, James," I hear a familiar woman's voice say to me from a long, long, *long* ways away.

"I found one!" Lana yells out, displaying a perfectly happy and toothy smile. No bloody gaps. "A four-leaf clover!" She shows it off, a ray of sunshine slipping through the branches and illuminating the little four-pronged lucky charm in her hand.

"Do you want to put it in the stream and follow it?" she asks.

"Sure!"

Together we push through the willow branches and into the sunlight, running, running...

...as a beautiful bundle of white fur bounds through the tall grass with us...

...and we run, run, run...

...into the brilliant bright light in the sky.

The End

About J.R. Rain:

J.R. Rain is the international bestselling author of over seventy novels, including his popular Samantha Moon and Jim Knighthorse series. His books are published in five languages in twelve countries, and he has sold more than 3 million copies worldwide.

Please find him at: www.jrrain.com.